Crimson
Magic Clan,
Let's &
Go!!

KONOSUBA:
GOD'S BLESSING ON THIS
WONDERFUL WORLD!
5!

"...I take my eyes off you for one second, and look what you do!"

CAT EARS

猫耳

Kazuma

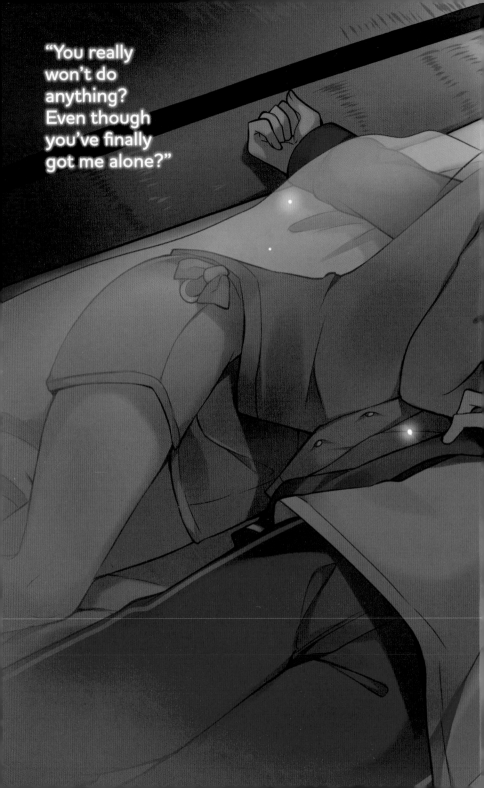

"You really won't do anything? Even though you've finally got me alone?"

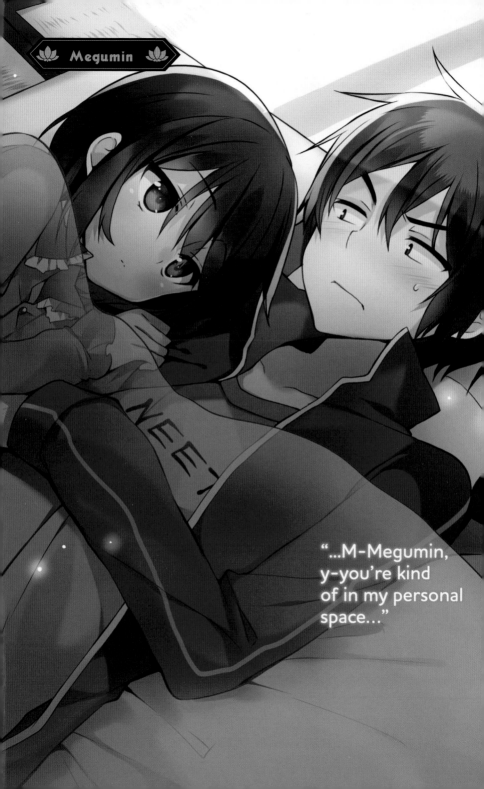

Darkness

"All right, you! If you're really minions of the Demon King, then prove it! Overpower me! Make me call you Master or something!"

KONOSUBA: GOD'S BLESSING ON THIS WONDERFUL WORLD! 5

Crimson Magic Clan, Let's & Go!!

CONTENTS

KONOSUBA: GOD'S BLESSING ON THIS WONDERFUL WORLD!

Crimson Magic Clan, Let's & Go!!

NATSUME AKATSUKI

ILLUSTRATION BY
KURONE MISHIMA

YEN
ON
NEW YORK

KONOSUBA: GOD'S BLESSING ON THIS WONDERFUL WORLD! 5

NATSUME AKATSUKI

Translation by Kevin Steinbach
Cover art by Kurone Mishima

KONO SUBARASHII SEKAI NI SHUKUFUKU WO!, Volume 5: BAKURETSU KOMA NI LET'S & GO!!
Copyright © 2014 Natsume Akatsuki, Kurone Mishima
First published in Japan in 2014 by KADOKAWA CORPORATION, Tokyo.
English translation rights arranged with KADOKAWA CORPORATION, Tokyo, through TUTTLE-MORI AGENCY, INC., Tokyo.

English translation © 2018 by Yen Press, LLC

Yen On
1290 Avenue of the Americas
New York, NY 10104

Visit us at yenpress.com
facebook.com/yenpress
twitter.com/yenpress
yenpress.tumblr.com
instagram.com/yenpress

First Yen On Edition: April 2018

Yen On is an imprint of Yen Press, LLC.
The Yen On name and logo are trademarks of Yen Press, LLC.

The publisher is not responsible for websites (or their content) that are not owned by the publisher.

Library of Congress Cataloging-in-Publication Data
Names: Akatsuki, Natsume, author. | Mishima, Kurone, 1991– illustrator. | Steinbach, Kevin, translator.
Title: Konosuba, God's blessing on this wonderful world! / Natsume Akatsuki ; illustration by Kurone Mishima ; translation by Kevin Steinbach.
Other titles: Kono subarashi sekai ni shukufuku wo. English
Description: First Yen On edition. | New York, NY : Yen On, 2017–
Identifiers: LCCN 2016052009 | ISBN 9780316553377 (v. 1 : paperback) |
ISBN 9780316468701 (v. 2 : paperback) | ISBN 9780316468732 (v. 3 : paperback) |
ISBN 9780316468763 (v. 4 : paperback) | ISBN 9780316468787 (v. 5 : paperback) |
Subjects: | CYAC: Fantasy. | Future life—Fiction. | Adventure and adventurers—Fiction. |
BISAC: FICTION / Fantasy / General.
Classification: LCC PZ7.1.A38 Ko 2017 | DDC [Fic]—dc23
LC record available at https://lccn.loc.gov/2016052009

ISBNs: 978-0-316-46878-7 (paperback)
978-0-316-46879-4 (ebook)

10 9 8 7 6 5 4 3 2 1

LSC-C

Printed in the United States of America

KONOSUBA: GOD'S BLESSING ON THIS WONDERFUL WORLD!

Crimson Magic Clan, Let's & Go!!

Wondering about a certain town? Wonder no more!
CRIMSON MAGIC VILLAGE: ETERNAL GUIDE

Descriptions & pictures: Arue

SIGHTSEEING GUIDE

Even the Demon King fears our Crimson Magic Village, but you don't have to fear our plethora of fine tourist destinations! There are powerful magic creatures in the wilderness—so take caution when making your trip!

▶ Wishing Pond

Holy pond. Offer an ax to summon the goddess of gold and silver or toss in a coin to make your wish come true!

▶ Stone with a Sword in It

A legendary sword is lodged in this rock. It's said whoever pulls it out will be given great power.

▶ Public Bath "Mixed Bath"

A dynamic hot bath where the owner uses Create Water to keep the tub full and Fireball to heat it.

▶ The Deadly Poison Café

Features food as fine as its name. One of several must-see shops adored by fans of the village, along with our armor shop, Goblin Slayer.

Check it out! The Crimson Magic Village is full of top Arch-wizard talents. Who knows? Maybe the one to defeat the Demon King will come from this very town!

Diagram of Crimson Magic Village School

One-on-One Interview with "Crimson Magic Village School's Number One Genius"!

Correct.
I am the number one genius at Crimson Magic Village School.
I seek to be the strongest. I have no interest in mere advanced magic.

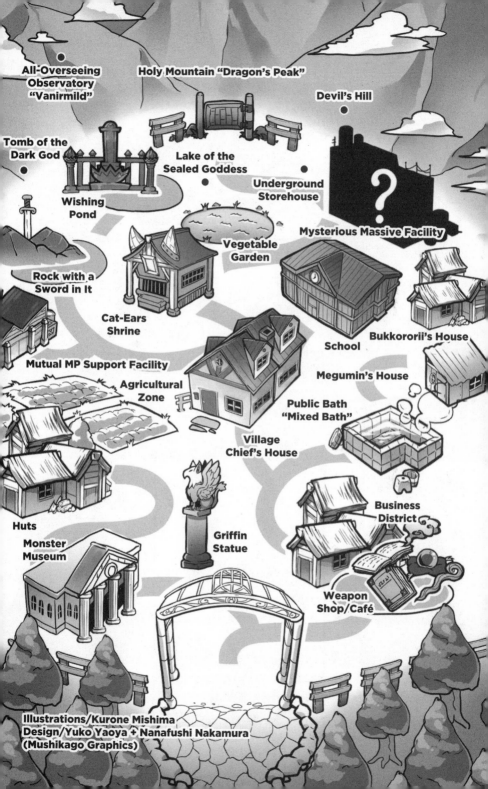

All-Overseeing Observatory "Vanirmild"

Holy Mountain "Dragon's Peak"

Devil's Hill

Tomb of the Dark God

Lake of the Sealed Goddess

Underground Storehouse

Wishing Pond

Mysterious Massive Facility

?

Vegetable Garden

Rock with a Sword in It

Cat-Ears Shrine

School

Bukkororii's House

Mutual MP Support Facility

Megumin's House

Agricultural Zone

Public Bath "Mixed Bath"

Village Chief's House

Huts

Business District

Monster Museum

Griffin Statue

Weapon Shop/Café

Illustrations/Kurone Mishima
Design/Yuko Yaoya + Nanafushi Nakamura
(Mushikago Graphics)

Characters

Darkness

Age 18
Job Crusader

A female knight who specializes in defense and enjoys being beaten up by monsters. Daughter of the Dustiness family, a powerful noble house. Special skill: fantasizing.

Aqua

Age Unknown
Job Arch-priest

A goddess who gives guidance to the young and deceased. Goes to a parallel world with Kazuma to defeat the Demon King. Likes wine. Special skill: party tricks.

Megumin

Age 14
Job Arch-wizard

Exceptionally talented, even by Crimson Magic Clan standards. Obsessed with the überpowerful spell Explosion, she is neither capable of nor interested in using any other magic. Favorite thing: Explosion. Special skill: Explosion. Hobby: Explosion.

Wiz

Age 20
Job Shopkeeper

Yunyun

Age 13
Job Arch-wizard

Kazuma Satou

Age 16
Job Adventurer

An adventurer and *hikikomori* (in any world) who brought Aqua to their current plane. Has already given up on defeating the Demon King.

Vanir

Age Unknown
Job Terrible demon, shopkeeper

Chomu-suke

Age ???
Job ???

Prologue

"Explosion!!"

A massive fireball tore through the formerly tranquil plain, accompanied by a whoosh and rumble that whipped up a gigantic dust cloud. I went over to where Megumin, now fresh out of MP, lay collapsed on the ground.

"H-how many points was that...?" she asked. As drained as she obviously was, the light in her eyes hadn't dimmed.

"Based on reverberation and destructive power, I'd say...eighty-five points!"

"Ah, I would expect no less from you, Kazuma. If I were to rate that explosion myself, I would give it much the same score. What a connoisseur you've become...!"

"Heh-heh! I like to think I've learned a thing or two, doing this with you every single day. You may refer to me as your *explosier*—like a sommelier, except with explosions. Come on, climb aboard." Megumin gave a tired groan as I hefted her onto my shoulders. "So you really never get sick of explosions, huh? Never think maybe it's about time you picked up some other spells and changed classes to 'Great Wizard'?"

"No, never. In fact, I do not even understand what you're saying, because I am already a great wizard."

The self-proclaimed "great wizard" was running her hands along my back. Thinking about it, I guess she had actually been sort of helpful recently, as long as she used her skills at the right time. With a sigh, I made sure she was safely settled.

Tomorrow, we'll be on the road again.

Megumin had talked me into going out for her daily explosion on the grounds that once we were traveling, she might need to conserve her MP and not be able to use her magic.

It was true. She really didn't get sick of explosions.

We headed for Axel Town with the twilight sun glowing red on the horizon. Behind me, Megumin was muttering stubbornly.

"Next time, I'll get a hundred points for sure…!"

May There Be Resolution Because of This Grave Letter!

1

—I want to bear your children.

I froze, tea dribbling from my lips. Yunyun sounded so passionate.

She stood trembling in front of me, her face red and her fists clenched. It looked like I wasn't the only one who couldn't move. Everyone else stood with their mouths hanging open, too. How could they not after such a declaration?

"Hey, Megumin, could I make a different move? If you let me take it back, I'll give you this weird-shaped rock I found in the bath at Arcanletia…"

No, I take it back. One person *was* ignoring our conversation, completely out of touch. Across from the stiffened Megumin, Aqua was holding one of her pieces and fretting.

I collected myself and wiped the tea from my mouth. In her astonishment, Darkness had let her cup tilt too far, spilling tea all over the rug.

I put my own drink on the table, straightened my collar, and turned to Yunyun.

"…What did you just say?" I asked.

Burning red, she replied, "I—I said I want to bear your children!"

Guess I didn't mishear.

"…Personally, I want a girl first," I said.

"N-no! A boy! It has to be a boy first!" she said.

Gosh, and here I thought Yunyun seemed like the quiet, submissive type. I guess she wasn't afraid to speak her mind after all. But there were some things even I couldn't bend on. A man wants to hear his daughter call him "Dad"...!

Megumin seemed to come to, because she suddenly stood up. "Now wait just a minute! Who cares whether it's a girl or a boy?! How are we even talking about that already? Yunyun! What in the world has gotten into you? Do you even know what you're saying?!"

"Sh-she's right! Yunyun, was it? Listen to Megumin! I don't know what happened between you and Kazuma, but don't let him mislead you! Do you know what kind of man he is?!"

There went Darkness, impugning my reputation.

"Huh? Hang on a second! Yes, that's it! If I take this Crusader I thought I didn't need and move her here...!"

Aqua was still completely oblivious to the commotion, off in her own little world with her game pieces. Her opponent, Megumin, was busy shaking Yunyun by the shoulders.

"Please, recover your sanity! Then again, I know how you sometimes charge ahead, blind to what's around you! I beg you to tell us what is going on—slowly and clearly!"

Yunyun, on the verge of tears under Megumin's shaking, yelped, "W-well! Well! Y-you know! If Kazuma and I don't have a child, the whole world will—! The Demon King will—!"

"I see," I said, "this is about the world, is it? Never fear. Say no more. Leave the world and the Demon King to me. Yunyun and I just have to have a child, and that will somehow take care of the Demon King and save the world—is that right? Well, far be it from me to deny the pleas of the distraught."

"Why, you impossible—! I recall you fighting us tooth and nail when we wanted to go on a quest the other day!"

"Indeed! Why would you choose now of all times to start having a heart? In fact, perhaps you *should* have some doubts about such an out-of-the-blue plot development!"

"Keep it to yourselves," I told the two interlopers. "What's with you guys, anyway? This is between Yunyun and me, and we don't need any kibitzers. I'm finally getting popular with the ladies—so butt the hell out!"

"Look who's talking! I mean—I am not a kibitzer! My friend is getting involved with some weird guy. How can I not say something?"

Megumin was having none of it, so I returned fire.

"I've spent every minute in this world surrounded by gorgeous younger women *and* gorgeous older women, and nothing has happened! How's that for weird? Aren't we heroes who've conquered general after general of the Demon King? Solved every problem we've come up against? The girls should be lining up for me by now! Adventurers should be begging for my autograph! Hey, Darkness! If you're really nobility, how about you get me an award or something for all my great deeds?"

"H-hey! Don't say that! It doesn't count if you're the one calling your deeds great!"

Yunyun, watching our argument heat up, finally panicked and jumped in. "E-everyone, please calm down! I'm sorry! I started this— please, just take it easy."

"I heard it was normal around here for people to get married between the ages of sixteen and twenty! And that you can get married as young as fourteen or something! Megumin, if Yunyun was a classmate of yours, she must be fourteen already, right? Then there's no problem! Perfect, it's perfect! Oh, the joy of not running afoul of the law! Oh, the freedom from accusations of liking one too young! I think I might actually be starting to like this world! Or what? Did you guys want me? Do you feel the flames of jealousy burning now that Yunyun and I are an item? Then come out and say it, you stupid passive-aggressive—!"

"Why, you—! Darkness! Let's get him! I want to wring his scrawny little neck!"

"You got it! Let's teach him to keep his mouth shut, permanently!"

"Oh, you wanna go, huh? Don't forget, I've got Drain Touch. So wherever I touch you, it's legitimate self-defense! Not sexual harassment!"

I waved my hand threateningly at them, and Megumin raised her eyebrow. And just as it looked like she was about to attack—there was a tug on her cape.

"Come on, Megumin, it's your turn. Look at this—I'm super-proud of this move. Come on, get over here!"

"Explosion!"

"Eeeyikes!"

Before Aqua could give her cape another tug, Megumin shouted "Explosion!" and flipped over the game board without even looking.

"Aww... We really need to ban the Explosion Rule," Aqua said, picking up the pieces now littering the carpet. Megumin ignored her, instead jabbing her staff in my direction.

"I strive every day to become the strongest of all wizards. Whereas you, Kazuma, have miserable stats. Even without using magic, I shall defeat you easily!"

"All right, now I'm feeling it. You know the best thing about me? Despite those crummy stats, I've still managed to defeat a whole list of powerful bad guys. I don't plan on breaking that streak for **one Explosion-obsessed moron**. And that **muscle-headed Crusader** over there? As if."

"Muscle-headed Crusader?!"

It looked like war was about to break out when Yunyun, teary-eyed, exclaimed:

"Megumin, listen to me! **Crimson Magic Village—our home—is going to be destroyed!**"

2

"It's not much, but have this tea."

"Th-thank you very much." Seated on the sofa as she accepted the cup from Aqua, Yunyun finally seemed to have calmed down a little.

"Now, what is this all about?" Megumin asked. "I am not pleased to hear our village is going to be destroyed. Could you kindly explain?"

Numbly, Yunyun passed her an envelope. Megumin pulled out a two-page letter and began to read.

By the time this letter reaches you, I will be dead. It appears that the army of the Demon King, which so long feared our power, is finally preparing a serious invasion. A massive military base has already been established near the village. But that is not all.

Beside the multitude of minions, a general with strong resistance to magic has been dispatched.

Heh-heh. That wily Demon King—he really is afraid. With no chance of destroying the base, our options are limited.

That's right. As chief of the Crimson Magic Clan, it is my duty to duel the general of the Demon King's army, even if it costs me my life.

My beloved daughter. As long as you are left, the blood of the Crimson Magic Clan shall not run dry. I leave you my place as chief of our clan. You are the last of the Crimson Magic Clan in this world. Do not let it die out...

"A letter from your father, Yunyun? The clan chief? **'By the time this letter reaches you, I will be dead'**?" Megumin's expression darkened little by little as she ran her eyes over the message. Its contents were enough to upset anyone. The Demon King's army had set up shop right near Crimson Magic Village, with the general and plenty of subordinates in tow. And apparently, it wasn't just any general, but one who could withstand magic. And at that moment, the village had no hope of eliminating the army's base...

The letter explained that, for the honor of Crimson Magic Village, the clan's leader would go out and do battle with the Demon King's general. And...

"**'I leave you my place as chief of our clan. You are the last of the Crimson Magic Clan in this world. Do not let it die out...'** Just a moment!" Megumin said, thoroughly annoyed. "I can assure you there is at least one other surviving member of the Crimson Magic Clan!"

"Never mind that!" Yunyun said. "Keep reading! There's another page."

On the day the village fortune-teller predicted the town's destruction by the army of the Demon King, she also glimpsed a ray of hope. She foresaw that Yunyun, the lone survivor of the Crimson Magic Clan, would set off to train in hopes of defeating the Demon King. In a starter town, she would meet a certain man. Irresponsible and totally powerless though this man was, he would become her partner in life...

Yunyun would take this worthless layabout under her precious wing. After spending all her time training, she would have little money, but she would be happy.

And time would pass.

The child born of the survivor of the Crimson Magic Clan and the man she met would grow into a young man. He would follow in the footsteps of his adventurer father, setting out on a journey. But he would not know—he himself would be the one to bring low his clan's age-old enemy, the Demon King...

Chronicle of the Hero of the Crimson Magic Clan, Chapter 1—by Arue

"'**On the day the village fortune-teller predicted the town's destruction by the army of the Demon King, she also glimpsed a ray of hope. She foresaw that Yunyun, the lone survivor of the Crimson Magic Clan...**' Once again, why are you the lone survivor of our clan? What do they think has happened to me?!"

"Shut up and keep reading," I snapped.

"'**...Yunyun, the lone survivor of the Crimson Magic Clan, would set off to train in hopes of defeating the Demon King. In a starter town, she would meet a certain man. Irresponsible and totally powerless though this man was, he would become her partner in life.**'"

Aqua, Darkness, and Megumin were all staring at me.

"Hey, what's everyone looking at me for? What, you think I'm this irresponsible, totally powerless guy? Yunyun, don't tell me you came here because of that?"

Yunyun glanced away.

"Okay, I'll keep reading now. '**...And time would pass. The child born of the survivor of the Crimson Magic Clan and the man she met would grow into a young man. He would follow in the footsteps of his adventurer father, setting out on a journey. But he would not know—he himself would be the one to bring low his clan's age-old enemy, the Demon King...**'"

"'''''?!'''''"

I wasn't the only one who caught my breath at that. Aqua and Darkness gulped, too.

"M-my kid is gonna...?"

"W-wait just a second! This is completely out of left field! Come on, Kazuma, you're way too much of a skeptic to buy into something like fortune-telling, right?"

"This is real trouble! This is real trouble for *me*!"

While I stood there agape at the vastness of the destiny that had been entrusted to me, Darkness and Aqua seemed upset about something.

Hold on. They can't actually be jealous, can they? Wh-what, seriously?
Aqua was putting the *bitter* in this bittersweet moment.

"I don't have that kind of time! I need to defeat the Demon King *now*! Wait until Kazuma's kid grows up?! How long will that take? When can you call someone a young man, anyway? Not until he's, like, three years old, right? Please, let's just pretend this little prophecy never happened!"

Or maybe it was just all bitter now.

Anyway, did she want to send a baby to defeat the Demon King?

"We have a very talented fortune-teller in our village! So this prophecy..."

"You're right. Leave it to me. I'll do what I have to do to save the world."

"Y-you impossible man!" Darkness shouted. "Is this really what you want?! In all the time I've known you, you've never been able to make a snap decision—why today?!"

She had me by the collar and was bringing her face way too close to mine when Megumin suddenly remarked, "There is one more line to this letter. It says, '**Chronicle of the Hero of the Crimson Magic Clan, Chapter One—by Arue.**'"

""""?!""""

Darkness, Yunyun, and I all stopped and looked at her. Aqua peeked at the letter.

"Let me see that. Oh, hey, the handwriting is different from the first page. That must be a letter from Yunyun's dad. This page has a postscript. It says, '**P.S. Postage is expensive, so the chief let me use the same envelope as him. I'll send you chapter two when it's ready.**'"

"Aaaaaaaaahhhhh!!" Yunyun snatched the letter and threw it away. "Waaaaah! I can't believe this! Stupid, stupid Arueeeeee!"

Yunyun was throwing a tantrum on the floor, and I was completely lost. "Hey, someone explain what's going on here! Who or what is Arue, and what happened to my kid? What's the plan? You wanna do it right here, or should we go to my room?"

"Yes, you should go to your room," Megumin said, "and go to sleep.

Arue is a classmate of ours. She fancies herself a writer or something. She's…a bit strange."

Darkness looked immensely relieved. "Phew, so it was just a story? …Hmm? Hang on—what was that first page about, then?"

"I suppose it is probably true. The Demon King has wanted revenge against the Crimson Magic Clan since long ago, so it seemed likely he would show up one of these days. He must have finally decided to make a serious attempt against our village."

"Hey, what about the man over here? You got me all fired up and now—nothing? Yunyun! Yunyun and I were about to begin our torrid, bittersweet love affair…"

"No you weren't," Darkness said. "Seriously, you're in the way. Go hang out with Aqua or something. And Megumin, how can you be so calm? Aren't you worried about your family and your classmates? Your hometown is in a crisis!"

This caused Yunyun to look up from her weeping. "R-right!" she said. "This is no time for tears. Megumin, what are we going to do?! I think the village really is under attack. How can we help?!"

Megumin looked at the two girls. "We are the Crimson Magic Clan, which even the Demon King fears. I don't believe our people will be so easily subdued. And we have you with us, Yunyun—the chief's daughter. No matter what happens to the village, that means the clan will not die out. So think of it this way. The people of the village will forever be in our hearts—"

"You rat, Megumin! How can you be so detached all the time?!" Yunyun turned to me with tears in her eyes, her face flushed. "L-look, I… I'm sorry about that weird stuff I said. I mean, you're the only guy I know, and…"

"Y-yeah, sure. It's fine. The important thing is what we do next. Your home's in trouble, right?"

Yunyun wiped away her tears. "Yes. I plan to go back to Crimson Magic Village. After all, my…f-f… My f-f-friends…are…there…"

She could barely get the word *friends* out of her mouth. Maybe it wasn't the right one.

"Anyway, I'm sorry for the trouble, everyone. And Megumin, I'll… see you later, I guess."

And then she walked out the door, shoulders slumped. We watched her leave.

"…Kazuma, are you really just going to let her leave like that?" Darkness asked. "You were so hot and bothered and obsessed with showing off that I was sure you would say you'd go with her or something."

"They're under attack by the Demon King. If I went with her, I'd only get in the way. Plus, it's dangerous and scary, and we just got back from a trip, and it sounds like a pain to go on another one. But…I guess if Megumin is really worried about her, I'll have to try to help."

"Th-this from the man who normally cannot say enough about all the generals of the Demon King's army he's defeated! Anyway, why should I be worried about Yunyun? She is my rival, remember? Practically my enemy."

Megumin pointedly kept her back turned to us. Darkness and I smirked at her. We started whispering.

"Hey, for someone who hates her enemy so much, doesn't she seem pretty fidgety?"

"Quiet, Kazuma, Megumin knows herself. Maybe you should try to convince her…"

We finally earned a glare from Megumin.

"Hey, Aqua," I said, turning to her, "why don't you say…something…?"

"**Zzzzzzzz…**"

Aqua was on the couch, fast asleep.

I guess maybe all of this was too hard for her to follow.

…Eventually, Megumin went up to her bedroom, still sulking. Left in the living room, Darkness turned to me.

"Seriously though, Kazuma, are we just going to leave her? This girl Yunyun, isn't she Megumin's friend? I've heard she's strong, but…"

"Don't worry about it. She's a legitimate Crimson Magic Clan member. She can use advanced magic and everything. To be honest, she's probably safer by herself than with us bumbling along with her. Remember, our party includes an undead magnet, among other things." I shot a glance at Aqua, who was curled up on the couch with a trail of drool coming from her mouth.

Anyway, Megumin might be acting stubborn now, but it was only a matter of time…

—That night.

I had finished dinner and was lounging in my room when a hesitant knock came at my door.

"Come in!"

The person who entered in response to my invitation was, of course…

"…Kazuma. I would like to talk to you. Do you have a moment?"

Megumin stood there in her pajamas, working her mouth like she wanted to say something.

"Awfully late for a chat. You sure you didn't get all fired up fighting about Yunyun and come here to make up…physically?"

"I-I'll clock you for that! Ever since I turned fourteen, the sexual harassment has been nonstop with you!"

Megumin was red and sputtering. I sat cross-legged on my bed, waiting. I mean, I had a pretty good idea of what she was going to say…

Megumin cleared her throat. "I— Ahem. I couldn't care less about Yunyun. But in fact, I have a younger sister…"

I didn't say anything.

"And so, while I really do not care even a little bit about Yunyun, I am very concerned about my sis— What are you smirking at?!"

Megumin's bald-faced attempt to pretend she didn't care about her friend had brought the thinnest of smiles to my face.

3

The next morning, I was showing everyone a map of the area around Crimson Magic Village that I'd gotten at the Adventurers Guild.

"So that's the story. This hot-cold type said she wants to go home, so I'm thinking about a little excursion to the Crimson Magic Clan's town."

"Who are you calling hot-cold?! I told you, my sister…!"

I put a hand on Megumin's forehead to hold her at bay and kept talking.

"Word is that the village is currently engaged with the Demon King's forces. So here's the plan: we scope out the place from a distance, and if it looks as dangerous as the letter said, we go straight home. If we run into anything that even looks like the Demon King's army on the way there, we go straight home. Also, we do everything possible to avoid any battles with monsters. Sound good?"

"Another one of your delightfully pessimistic plans, Kazuma!" Aqua said. "Well, fine. We may have just gotten back from a different trip, but I'm willing to go save Megumin's hometown!" She clenched her fist in anticipation. Our recent string of victories over officers of the Demon King seemed to have given her an uncharacteristic confidence.

"Crimson Magic Village? That place is a paradise just bursting with powerful monsters. *And* it's under assault by the forces of the Demon King…! Ahh! What shall I do on the day when their numbers over-whelm me and I am captured? Listen, Kazuma, when that happens, forget about me! Think only of yourself!"

"Don't worry; I'll be more than happy to leave you behind. Don't follow us home, okay?" I shot down Darkness as her mind wandered off on another tangent. The three of us collected our luggage—we hadn't even unpacked from last time—and left the house.

Normally, we would have just headed for the carriage station, but I had a little plan in mind for this trip.

"Hey, Kazuma, where the heck are we going? Weren't we supposed to follow that Yunyun girl back to her village?"

"Yunyun left on a carriage just after noon yesterday. We'd never catch up. And I'm sick of carriage rides anyway. There's somewhere else I want to go."

Even as I answered Aqua, the little shop that was my destination came into view.

"...Erk. This is where you wanted to go? As... As a follower of Our Lady Eris, I'd rather avoid this place... I mean, it's..."

"Hello, hello, hello! Young man whose business experience sadly does not contribute to his level and young woman whose only worth lately has been the power of her family's name! And if it isn't our thug-slash-priest with her insufferable corona of light and the gimmicky clan member who knows only gimmick magic! You could not have come at a better time."

"...where this guy works!"

"Gimmicky clan member?!"

Darkness and Megumin took turns sounding put out as the employee wearing an uncanny mask greeted them from the corner of the store where he was cleaning. I had come here because I wanted to finish the business negotiations we had been putting off, and because there was something I wanted from Wiz...

Vanir swept around behind me, ushering me into the store. He crinkled his brow but otherwise ignored the flurry of quick little jabs courtesy of Aqua. I didn't see Wiz anywhere. But I did hear a quiet sniffling from somewhere inside...

Her unsettling employee kept pushing me along.

"What do you mean? Have you got something weird in stock again? Let's be clear: I'm not here to buy anything."

"Now, now, don't say that. I know some of my wares have been less than satisfactory, but even I have my moments. I have something I'm sure you'll be very interested in." Now that he had us inside, Vanir held out a small box with the lid open.

"…? What's this?"

"A magical item that repels the undead. Just open the lid, and a divine aura will keep them at bay for at least twelve hours. I recall you are accompanied by a most unusual someone of whom the undead are especially fond. In fact, I believe it made your life rather difficult on your recent excursion. If you had one of these, you could sleep in your bed or in the fields or anywhere with complete peace of mind!"

"Hang on, 'most unusual'? You're not talking about me, are you?"

Undead repellent, huh? I had to admit it sounded useful on the surface…

"And what's the catch? Don't pretend there isn't one."

"Oh, but there isn't. I suppose—well, the price might be considered a *little* high for a consumable, but that's it. It's very effective! I just keep this lid open, and our fog-brained shop owner can't come out of the back room. She's been in there crying all day—it's that good!"

"You mean that's Wiz I've been hearing this whole time? Put that thing away! Why did she even order something like that? …Tell you what, though, it does sound like it would be good to have around. Give me one. I'll be needing it right away." I pulled out my wallet, thinking about the camping we'd likely have to do.

"Always a pleasure doing business! One undead repellent. That will be one million eris!"

"That's highway robbery! At that price, I should just fight the damn zombies!"

Vanir ignored me, assiduously putting a new box into a bag for us.

"Why worry, my honored customer? After all, you're going to be a rich man soon! I'll buy the intellectual property rights to all your inventions thus far for three hundred million eris! Does this agreement look acceptable to you?" He pulled out a contract as he spoke.

"Three hundred million eris…! If he got that kind of money, he'd never work again! He'd become a worthless lump! But then again, even that might not be so bad…" Beside me, Darkness looked worried. I'm sure I had no idea what she was muttering about.

On either side of me, Aqua and Megumin were tugging on my sleeves, wearing ingratiating smiles.

"Kazuma! My dear Kazuma. I dream of having a pool in our house…"

"I want to get an MP Purifier Machine. It is supposed to aid in the recovery of Magic Points."

"Oof, nothing like a whiff of money to bring out the gold diggers. Pools and magic purifiers sound really expensive, and I'm not rich yet. For now, go see if you can find any items we might need for this trip."

At my urging, the two of them happily began rooting through the shop's item collection.

For my part, I decided to take the lump sum for the rights to my intellectual property. With my propensity for getting caught up in risky goings-on, I figured it was best to take the money and run while I had the chance. In a single year, there had been two separate incidents in this town—a high-ranking Demon King general and a mobile fortress. You couldn't be too careful.

"Okay, just take the cost of that undead repellent thing out of my three hundred mil. I'm assuming I won't be able to get the money right away?"

"Sadly, no. The woebegone working-Lich weeping in the back room had to go and order these ridiculous things—that means outlay is in short supply. To put it bluntly, we have no money. Oh, don't make that face. I will have plenty of capital next week—I've invited investors to come to town."

Next week, huh? Starting next week, I would be the town's richest man!

"Oh, now that you mention it, I wanted to talk to Wiz. Could you go get her?"

With a hangdog expression, Vanir closed the lid of the box that had been releasing a white mist into the air. He opened a window to clear out the place, and finally Wiz emerged from the back room. She smiled and welcomed us. Until just recently, the exertions of our trip to

Arcanletia had left her with one foot in the next life, but now she looked back to her normal, deathly pale self.

"Hey, Wiz, feeling better? Sorry to keep bothering you. We're not really here to shop today—I've got a favor to ask you."

"...? A favor? Me?"

I nodded. I told her what was going on in Megumin's village and explained exactly what I wanted.

"I see," she said at length. "So you just need me to Teleport everyone to Arcanletia?"

To reach Crimson Magic Village, first we would have to go through Arcanletia. And this Lich, who for an undead was awfully fond of baths, had fallen in love with the city on our trip and set it as one of the destinations of her Teleport spell.

While Wiz and I were talking, everyone else had been looking over her stock.

"H-hey, Vanir. What's this 'monster-attractant potion'? If you were to, you know, smear this all over your body, what would happen?"

"That potion is intended to be administered orally. When you drink it, I guarantee not only monsters but townspeople, relatives, even your own friends will attack you out of a sudden hatred. I should think it would be very much suited to your—*ahem*—preferences. You'll take one?"

"...Even my family and friends will hate me...? Hrm. I can't have them hating me forever, but depending on the duration of the effect, maybe..."

"...Oh-ho. This says here that these potions temporarily strengthen the effect of a specific magic spell. Do you have any that make Explosion more potent?"

"Mm. The only booster potions we have in stock at the moment are for binding magic and swamp magic. The Bind booster potion increases the spell's area of effect, so you become as paralyzed as your enemy. The swamp booster likewise makes the effect larger, so the caster is among those who drown."

"Well, that will not do." Megumin turned her attention to another product. "What is this strangely lifelike doll?"

"That's a Vanir doll. A fine piece of work that contains a shard of my own mask to scare away evil spirits. It's currently the only product that's actually selling. Granted, it cackles in the middle of the night, but it certainly does its job. What about you lot? There are no evil spirits in your house, but you do have a spectral resident. Want to try one?"

"It cackles at night?" Megumin said. "And this is supposed to assure you that there *aren't* evil spirits around? Anyway, Aqua would never sit by if there was a ghost in our house."

"Megumin, didn't you believe what I said? I told you—the ghost of a little noblegirl lives in that mansion! I haven't cleared her out yet because I felt bad for her. I'm just letting her enjoy herself!"

"Oh yes. I remember. This is the 'ghost' who drinks all your wine?"

"You, too, Darkness? Aww, please believe me!"

Geez, what a noisy bunch...

As I tried to tune out what was going on behind me, Wiz had a dreamy look on her face.

"You know, I visited Crimson Magic Village for some acquisitions once. I went to call on a very famous magical-item merchant named Hyoizaburou, but unfortunately, he wasn't in..."

Almost instantaneously, Megumin appeared at my side with a little yelp of shock.

"E-excuse me, but did you say 'Hyoizaburou'? Th-that is, how long ago did you go to the village?"

"That would have been...about two years ago, I guess? Oh yeah—when I went to his house, a pretty girl answered the door. She looked a lot like you, Miss Megumin..."

At that, Megumin grabbed her head and curled up into a ball.

"What's the deal?" I asked. "Something wrong?"

"N-no... My rash decision seems to have cost him his business..."

As I was trying to fathom what Megumin was talking about, sounds of a struggle came from behind me.

"Don't touch my products, you menace! If you lay a finger on my potions, they'll turn to water!"

"That's some way to talk! I thought customers were supposed to be treated like deities! Speaking as an actual goddess, I should know! So how about a little less sass and a little more groveling?"

"You're a pathetic deity and a terrible customer! How dare you give me lip when you go around making my stock worthless! Hey, Wiz! I heard what you were saying. Hurry up and teleport these troublemakers before they do any more damage!"

Wiz gave a helpless smile at Vanir's tirade and began preparing her spell.

"Hey, kid." Vanir leaned in toward me as I watched Wiz work. "Let the all-seeing demon give you a word of advice—my way of thanking you for a pricey purchase." He took a breath. "Once you reach your destination, a time will come when one of your companions will confide in you about some confusion. What you say may change the path that person takes in life. Think carefully and be sure the advice you offer will leave no regrets."

Gosh, that sounds awfully important. Even if his "advice" is terribly suspicious.

I ended Aqua's endless stream of complaints, and the four of us gathered in one spot.

"All right then, everyone," Wiz said. "I wish you a safe journey! *Teleport!*"

4

I found myself squeezing my eyes shut as Wiz cast her spell. When I opened them again, Arcanletia, "the city of water and hot springs," was there in front of us. I hadn't expected to ever come back here—let alone almost immediately after we'd left.

"Hey, Kazuma! Kazuma, hey!"

"Oh no. We're not staying here a minute longer than we have to. I don't want anything to do with your followers."

"Aww, what is your problem?"

We decided to stick around long enough to try to get some information from Yunyun, as well as to placate Aqua, who, perhaps naturally, was eager to stay a night.

Yunyun had left the previous day. She must have gone by carriage, but even so, the distance from Axel to Arcanletia couldn't be covered in a day, even if you departed early in the morning. My guess was that Wiz's Teleport had gotten us here ahead of her.

…But when I suggested we wait and meet up with her, Megumin gave me a dour look.

"Kazuma, I am not going home out of concern for Yunyun. I am worried about my sister, as I told you. So I think we should move on immediately. Knowing Yunyun, she will have no trouble catching up to us."

So she was sticking to her story about her sister.

…*What a pain.*

In the end, we decided not to stay in Arcanletia and set off for Crimson Magic Village instead. Personally, I was just as happy to be out of reach of the Axis Church's crazy "missionaries." But then again, the road to the village was supposed to be so dangerous that even merchant caravans wouldn't use it. The Crimson Magic Clan members themselves got around using Teleport. In other words, there was no need to risk losing a convoy for them.

We put Arcanletia behind us, heading for Crimson Magic Village along the road.

"It's about two days' walk from here to the village. There are a lot of dangerous monsters on the way, so we'll be relying on Kazuma's Sense Foe skill," Megumin said.

Frankly, I was terrified at the prospect of camping out with all those monsters around. I wanted to cover as much ground as we could while the sun was up.

"Leave it to me," I said. "I took care of a few little enemies on our last trip, remember? It actually made my level go up. I had plenty of skill points, so I picked up a thief skill called Flee. It allows you to escape battle at any time."

"Hey, doesn't that only affect you, Kazuma?" Aqua said. "Are you saying that anytime you sense an enemy, you can just run away by yourself? That's not what you're saying, is it?"

We trundled along with Darkness up front and Megumin, Aqua, and me behind. I was ignoring Aqua's uncharacteristically perceptive questions.

"Kazuma," Megumin said, "aren't Adventurers supposed to level up easily? We had that whole intense battle with the Demon King's general, and you only got one level? I jumped straight up to 33!"

"Hey, put that card away before I throw it away. It's not like I have a choice. You can take out the boss and all the small fry in the area in one big blast, but I have to make do with my bow and this sword with its weird name."

We were still arguing as we proceeded toward a forest—and Darkness stopped in her tracks.

"...Eep. There's someone there..."

I followed her gaze and saw a green-haired girl sitting on an outcropping of rock near the forest entrance. She was waving as if she'd just noticed us.

Is she here alone?

...Then my eyes went to her feet. Her right ankle was wrapped in blood-soaked bandages. The sight made me wince.

She was looking at us with upturned eyes. I felt one of my skills activate.

...What can I say?

Except...this world is really absolutely, positively no good!

"Aww, you're hurt. Are you okay?" Aqua was approaching the girl solicitously. I grabbed her shoulder, drawing a look not only from her but from Darkness and Megumin as well.

"My Sense Foe skill is tingling. That's a monster in disguise."

""""Huh?!"""""

I ignored the girl's imploring expression. While staying mindful of our surroundings, I pulled out the Guild's map of the road to Crimson Magic Village. It included information about the monsters you might meet on the way. I checked to see if any of them fit this girl's description...

There it is.

"Leisure Girl." That had to be her.

"Come on, Kazuma, she's looking at you all sad and stuff... I kind of can't help wanting to go cast Heal on her."

I refused to loosen my grip on Aqua's shoulder. Instead, I reviewed the info we had on this creature.

"Leisure Girl: This plant-type monster does not do direct physical damage. However, it will attempt to provoke strong protective feelings in passing travelers to lure them closer. Its advances are difficult to resist, and once you give in to your sympathy for it, you will remain its prisoner until you die. Some maintain that this monster is actually highly intelligent, but this is not certain. We request that adventuring groups who encounter this monster exterminate it, difficult as that may be."

"Kazuma, sh-she's looking at me," Darkness said, sounding unusually irresolute. "Look at those big round eyes! Are you sure it's a monster?"

"While travelers are near this monster, it will display a highly relaxing smile, making it difficult to leave. If an attempt to withdraw is nonetheless made, it will begin to cry. The more good-hearted the traveler, the more dangerous this monster is."

"K-Kazuma, that girl... She is waving 'bye-bye' to us and struggling to put on her bravest smile so as not to cry... Surely, one little hug would not hurt?"

I let go of Aqua and grabbed Megumin by the collar.

"Once ensnared, it will come closer to its prey, making it difficult to avoid. While hunger might normally prompt a traveler to move on, a further danger of this monster is that it will share its own fruit with such famished captives. The fruit is in fact quite

tasty. But it is almost entirely devoid of nutritional value, so one will continue to lose weight no matter how much one eats. Travelers suffer pangs of conscience to see the little girl offer them her own fruit, eventually cease to eat at all, and die of malnutrition."

"Hrk…! Even if it is a monster, to walk away from someone injured…!" Darkness couldn't stand it anymore; she started approaching the Leisure Girl. But since the map said the creature didn't do any physical damage, I let her go and kept reading.

"Some element in the Leisure Girl's fruit seems to interfere with the nervous system, because eventually hunger, fatigue, pain, and other danger signals cease to be sent to the body. As a result, the creature's prey enters a dreamlike state, wastes away, and dies. Some elderly adventurers, seeking a peaceful death, have deliberately gone to this monster's habitat, which is where it gets its name. After the death of its prey, the Leisure Girl puts down roots over the deceased traveler and draws nutrition from—"

…I stopped reading. Somewhere along the line, Megumin had escaped my grip and joined Aqua in walking toward the girl. All of them were aware it was a monster and not exactly eager to touch it quite yet, but they were definitely in kind of a daze.

The Leisure Girl looked at them with eyes full of fleeting hope: *You'll really stay with me?* My companions, their protective impulses stirred by her expression, were flexing their fingers in anticipation.

"It looks like this monster doesn't do physical damage," I said. "Instead, it plays on people's emotions and starves them to death before running its roots into them."

At my words, the three of them drew even closer to the Leisure Girl, wearing placid expressions. I had to wonder if they were listening to the part about being starved to death.

"I'll take care of your poor boo-boos!" Aqua said. But a moment later: "Huh? These aren't injuries at all. These aren't even bandages—just something that looks like them."

That prompted me to come take a closer look, too.

The Leisure Girl wore clothes like you might see on any young kid around town. She had bare feet and was smiling happily to have everyone clustering around her. When I got close, I realized the rock she was sitting on was part of her fake body, too. A branch-like thing extended from the back of it, and a small fruit was growing there. The clothes, the blood-soaked bandages—all of it was just a trick to get people to feel sorry for her.

What kind of monster would impersonate an injured little girl? I mean, come on.

That was what I was thinking, anyway. Beside me, my three companions were busy fussing over the Leisure Girl. Megumin held her hand out gently, and the creature looked at it with anxious eyes that said, *Can I really?*

She clasped the outstretched hand, and her face blossomed into an expression of pure bliss.

That seemed to be it for the three of them.

Crimson Magic Village might have been in danger, but this thing was its own kind of trouble. I thought back to the warning from the monster info. **"The more good-hearted the traveler, the more dangerous this monster is."** And: **"We request that adventuring groups who encounter this monster exterminate it, difficult as that may be."**

I stood in front of the Leisure Girl and drew my katana-ish sword, Chunchunmaru.

When Aqua saw me, she hugged the Leisure Girl protectively. "What are you doing, Kazuma?! You can't possibly mean to farm this sweet little girl for experience points, can you?"

Excuse me, but that's a monster. A deadly one.

Megumin, still holding the creature's hand, gazed at me beseechingly. "I, too, know of the Leisure Girl. But surely you wouldn't hurt a being in the form of such an adorable child? People say you are a demonic monster and morally bankrupt, but I know you also care about your friends and have the occasional moment of kindness. I know you wouldn't do something like this… Would you…?" You'd think she was pleading with her parents not to take the kitten she found to the animal shelter.

…Geez. I mean, it's not like I'm doing this for fun.

Darkness sensed my hesitation, but she seemed to remember that we were dealing with a monster. "…No," she said. "If Kazuma has decided to eliminate this thing, then that's what we should do. I went to it because I thought it was injured, but this monster doesn't have any wounds. That means this is all a cunning disguise. If we leave it here, who knows what kind of damage it will do down the line?" As she spoke, she drew her great sword, taking up a stance against the Leisure Girl.

At that, the Leisure Girl spoke in a voice so soft it was hard to hear, stumbling over her words like a child.

"…You're gonna…k-kill…me…?"

She clung to Megumin's hand and looked up at Darkness without ever leaving her rock. Tears welled in her eyes, and she started to tremble.

So it can talk…

Quaking so hard her great sword rattled, Darkness silently implored me with the exact same expression as the Leisure Girl.

Geez, you too? What am I supposed to do about this?

I pushed the immobilized Darkness out of the way, stepping forward with my sword in my hand. Aqua stood in front of the Leisure Girl to block me, shadowboxing to keep me at bay.

…Some goddess. Getting all chummy with a monster…

The Leisure Girl looked anxiously at Megumin, still holding her hand, and then gave me a terrified glance.

"…He's gonna…k-kill…me…?"

The sight of that questioning, teary-eyed look hit me somewhere deep in my heart. Three companions and one monster all watched me.

Keep it together! This monster took human lives. If we didn't do something about it, someone else might become its victim. Not to get all philosophical, but wouldn't letting it live be the greater evil?

Or would it be worse to kill it?

Grrrrrraaagh!

I stabbed my katana into the dirt, nearly pulling out my hair. Aqua, seeing the turmoil within me, said:

"Kazuma, when you're
confused like this,
whatever decision you
make is sure to leave
you full of regret. So
just take the path
of least resistance."

Thanks, that's just what a mature, responsible person would do. Not.

And anyway, everyone needed to just hold on a moment. There was one more reason I couldn't let the Leisure Girl go.

And that was Megumin's village.

We were headed straight into the jaws of the Demon King's army, his generals, and his minions. And while I had zero interest in fighting them, I wanted to get every level I could scrounge up—just in case. If the Leisure Girl lived here, in a country this dangerous, then it had to be worth some serious XP.

Darkness, Aqua, and Megumin all watched my internal battle. So did the Leisure Girl, wearing an uneasy look.

I had a good cause. If I didn't take out this monster, other people might get hurt.

...Gaaaaaaah, damn it all! I don't have any choice—forgive me! It might look like a person, but it's a monster! A monster! A monster...!

Seeing me stand there, apparently doomed to be locked in battle with myself forever, the Leisure Girl whispered, "You're in...pain. I'm sorry, it's...because I'm...alive, isn't it?" A smile flitted across her face. "I'm a...monster. I cause...trouble...just by being...alive." Tears began beading in her eyes. "This is the first...time in my...life...I've been able to talk...to a human." She brought her hands together in front of her chest, as if she was praying. "And it looks like...it will be the...last. I'm glad you...were the one I...talked to... If there is...such a thing as rebirth...I hope I won't...be a monster...in my next life."

...Sheesh. How could I kill *that*?

5

We continued on our way, leaving the Leisure Girl behind us.

Hey, don't judge me. I guess it might get someone in trouble later—but I don't value human life so highly that I could kill a monster that looks like a little girl and says things like that.

Sigh. I supposed she probably would get someone else passing through.

Even after we left, everyone acted as if something was tugging on them from behind. Aqua and Megumin would barely go forward, making my life difficult.

Aww, man! I feel bad leaving it, and I would have felt bad killing it. What a rude monster.

Then again, she did say this was the first time she had talked to a human. Maybe that meant she hadn't captured any other victims. So maybe letting her go was…the right choice…?

"Anyway, Kazuma, I'm so glad to learn you have a shred of humanity left in you," Aqua was saying. "I thought you were about to go, 'I'll make experience points out of you!' and then cast Kindle on her or something."

"We really need to have a talk about who exactly you think I am. You all knew I was never gonna do it, right?" I looked to Darkness and Megumin…

"…"

The two of them averted their eyes uncomfortably, not saying a word.

What I wouldn't give for companions kind and loving enough to understand me.

…Huh? "Hold on a second. I just realized how dangerous it is leaving that Leisure Girl on this road."

The thought of kind and loving companions had reminded me of Yunyun, who would be coming this way later. She had no friends, she was already the lonely type, and she was given to showing compassion to those around her. If she saw that thing…

The Leisure Girl had said we were the first humans she had talked to. That meant Yunyun definitely hadn't been by already.

"You look whiter than Wiz," Aqua said. "You have a stomachache? There are some bushes over there. Don't worry; we'll give you some space."

"You are so wrong! Look, you guys go on ahead. I need to talk to that Leisure Girl."

"What?! H-hey, Kazuma—?!"

With Aqua's confused shout ringing in my ears, I dashed back the way we had come.

6

It hadn't been five minutes since we'd left the Leisure Girl behind. If I ran, I would be there in no time. Then, as foolish as it might be, I would have to try to ask her not to bother the red-eyed girl who would be coming down this road—not even smile at her.

My mind kept spinning as I went. If I could get that concession from her, maybe I could even persuade her not to lure any travelers at all into her trap.

...Yes! That was it! I could ask the Axis Church in Arcanletia to send that sweet monster regular sustenance so it wouldn't have to attack anyone. I was going to be a gazillionaire when I got back to town anyway. I could spare enough to keep one monster fed. I was practically giddy with these thoughts as I went rushing back...!

When I got to where we had met the Leisure Girl, I could see she was talking with someone. I immediately activated my Ambush and Second Sight skills to check out what was going on.

She was speaking to a woodcutter. He must have lived in Arcanletia...

The woodcutter was advancing on her, ax in hand. Did he mean to kill her...? I slipped forward, leaving my Ambush skill active, trying to hear what he was saying.

His voice was all too clear. "Argh... Damn! I'm sorry! Forgive me! But we woodcutters know that if we find one of you, we have to get rid of you...!" He was practically weeping.

So he *was* going to kill her! I deactivated Ambush—

"I'm a...monster. I cause...trouble...just by being...alive."

—or I was about to, when I heard the creature speak...using the same words as before.

"This is the first…time in my…life…I've been able to talk…to a human."

The exact same words.

"And it looks like…it will be the…last. I'm glad you…were the one I…talked to. If there is…such a thing as rebirth…I hope I won't…be a monster…in my next life."

"Ahh! I can't do it!" the woodcutter exclaimed. "Damn it all, I just can't do it!" And then he turned and ran.

I stood dumbly in the shadow of the trees, not even turning off Ambush.

What's going on? Didn't she say *I* was the first human she had talked to?

"Pfah, there goes another one. And that woodcutter looked so meaty. There would have been plenty to feed on there…"

With the woodcutter gone, the Leisure Girl seemed to be talking to herself. She spoke in fluent, perfectly formed words.

I snuck around behind her and deactivated Ambush. The Leisure Girl didn't know I was there.

"Baaah… Shit. Come on, food, where are you? Maybe I'll have to settle for photosynthesis. And it's cloudy. What a pain in my ass…"

Still muttering, she lay down and stretched out as if to catch as much of the sun as she could…

…and her eyes met mine, as I stood directly behind her.

"…………"

For a very long moment, we looked at each other wordlessly. Then the Leisure Girl blurted, "Could…we p-pretend…that didn't…happen?"

"I know you can talk normal, you slimyyyy—!!"

When I got back to Aqua and the others, they were taking a break right where I'd left them. Maybe they'd been waiting for me.

Aqua smiled as I came running up. "Well, you look like there's a load off your mind! What happened? Something with you and that monster? What did you go back for, anyway?"

I gleefully showed her my Adventurer's Card. "Have a look at this! I just jumped *three* levels! That oughta do me some good when we reach Megumin's village."

The trio froze. Followed immediately by...

"Waa—waaaaaaaaaaaahhhh! Kazuma, you monster! You morally bankrupt demon! Now I see why Vanir likes you so much! You're worse than he is!"

"No... No... No, oh no... This is all my fault... If I hadn't bragged so much about all those levels I gained... If I hadn't teased Kazuma about it... Maybe that...poor thing...would still be alive! O damnable pride...!"

I was trying to get Aqua and Megumin to stop wailing long enough for me to explain when I registered Darkness standing stonily to one side. I gave her a quizzical look.

"It must have been painful," she said. "But you did your duty as an adventurer. Forgive us for making you bear this burden alone..."

Her expression was pained, and she was completely serious.

It took me a full hour to explain.

Chapter 2

May I Make a Harem of These Lustful Beast-Eared Girls!

1

As the curtain of night descended, we found a place by the side of the road. We cleared away the biggest rocks so it would be easy to sleep and laid out our sheet. It was about the size of a picnic blanket—and that was pretty much how we were using it.

We couldn't have the powerful monsters around here noticing a campfire, so instead we agreed to sleep huddled up in the dark. After I opened the undead repellent we'd bought from Vanir, we put everyone's provisions in the middle of the blanket, resting our backs against the pile.

We couldn't see the light of the stars, maybe because of the cloudy weather. But thanks to my Second Sight and Sense Foe skills, I could tell if a monster was coming even in the dark. That meant guard duty fell to me. And because I might have trouble dealing with the threat by myself, the others stood guard with me in turns. Megumin drew the first shift.

"...Kazuma, can you really stay up all night?" Darkness said from the gloom. "Granted, with your skill set, we appreciate your standing guard, but..."

"Don't worry about it. I've always been good at all-nighters. Where I come from, we pull them all the time."

"Now that you mention it, Kazuma, where *do* you come from?"

Megumin asked. "You and Aqua both. I'd love to hear about your home country. Based on your inventions, it's clearly a place with many useful magical items. I keep wondering what kind of life you lived there. What kind of life—what kind of sacrifices—awarded you such a talent for staying up all night...?"

I could feel Darkness looking at me, too, Megumin's words having piqued her interest.

What kind of life I lived, huh...?

I thought back on my peaceful life in Japan. Sitting and talking at night like this reminded me of school trips. The nostalgia was almost too much to bear. I slowly began to speak.

"Let's see... Well, I really owned in that world."

"'Owned'? Owned what?'" Megumin and Darkness said together.

I see they don't have that word in this world.

"I guess it means, you know, someone at the top of the pile. My friends had a bunch of nicknames for me. '**Kazuma, the guy with all the luck.**' '**Kazuma, the guy who's always there if you overdo it.**' That sort of thing... They really depended on me. My buddies and I would assault fortresses and take down huge bosses. Man, it was a good time... All-nighters? All the time. Didn't eat well, slept two hours a day, then it was off on another monster hunt."

Darkness sucked in an admiring breath next to me. "Th-that's amazing... Fortresses and bosses...! No wonder you always come up with good ideas, with all that experience. That's really something!" She sounded excited, full of genuine respect.

Even Megumin got in on it. "I would not normally believe such talk from you, Kazuma, but somehow... Somehow it just feels like you're telling the truth. I really do sense confidence and fondness for such memories from you..."

Then, from directly behind me, Aqua spoke up.

"...Hey, Kazuma. When do I get to tell them that you're talking about some online game?"

"Never. Please?"

2

Darkness told me that if anything happened, I should wake her up—I could be a little rough if I wanted to, she said—and I agreed I would find an *awful* way of alerting her if she was needed. Then Megumin and I went on guard duty.

"...You know, I have to wonder just what this awful way of waking someone up is. You know, there is a certain line you should not cross with your party members. You understand that, don't you?"

"Let me tell you something about men, Megumin. When you say there's a line we can't cross or a wall we can't climb, that makes us want to cross it or climb it more than ever... The bigger the obstacles in our lives, the higher the mountains we have to climb, the more we want to face them down! It's like that."

"No, it isn't! Please don't act like we are talking about something optimistic and motivational here! I'm not sure I feel safe being on guard duty with you..."

Megumin's agitated outburst provoked some groggy sleep-talk from Aqua.

"" ......""

The two of us went quiet, not wanting to wake her. I let out a small sigh of relief when I heard her breathing calmly and evenly again.

"By the way," Megumin started in a soft voice. "Going back to what we were talking about before bed..." She went on hesitantly. "You come from another country, don't you? ...Do you never go back home?"

"Truth is, even if I wanted to, I couldn't. And if I did go back, I'd probably end up being a lazy bum again. Just recently, I've started to think maybe this life isn't so bad. When we come back from Crimson Magic Village, I'll get the three hundred million eris from Vanir and be a rich man. Then we can all be lazy bums, just enjoying ourselves."

Being a NEET here wasn't so different from being a NEET in Japan. It seemed like it was mostly a question of whether you were a burden on your parents. Japan had video games, and computers, too, but it didn't have succubus services. Those seemed like the major differences.

Defeating the Demon King and going back to Japan?

It had started to seem like a pretty impossible idea. And anyway, sure, I wanted to see my parents again, but I was good and dead in Japan...

If I brought down the Demon King, I could wish for anything I wanted. Maybe I could get something better.

Megumin gave a small sigh of relief at my words.

"I see... I like this life, too. Exactly as it is. The way we all get in trouble but then somehow find a way out—it's a fun way to live, and it's enough for me."

I was about to ask how getting in trouble all the time counted as "fun" when she said:

"I hope all of us will always
be together like this."

She let out a small breath as she slid closer to me. She squeezed my hand in the darkness. Her own hand felt cold.

Why am I so nervous?

Wait, what the hell? This is some bittersweetness right here!

What was with this girl? Why had Megumin suddenly taken my hand without any context? First Yunyun wanted to have a baby with me, and now this? Maybe I really was finally getting popular with the ladies.

Memories of my romantic life flashed before my eyes. The first girl I had ever loved. How, in grade school, we had promised to get married when we grew up. How, in the summer of our third year of middle school, I saw her riding with a ne'er-do-well upperclassman on his motorbike. How, full of feelings I couldn't explain, I stopped going to school so much and lost myself in online games instead. How I didn't even want to sleep after that—just kill monsters until the sun came up. How eventually I had reached such heights that more people had heard of me than not...

I had spent the best years of my life training in online games. I had wasted the days when I was supposed to be enjoying the blossoming of romance at school. And now here I was, with a beautiful girl practically pressed up against me, my hand in hers.

Yikes. What was a guy supposed to do in this situation? Was she telling me to make a move on her? Should I say something suave? I had never thought much about Megumin in that way, and I didn't have any romantic feelings for her now, either—I mean, she was still too young. But didn't she realize that a virgin with zero experience with women wouldn't be able to just shake it off when a girl did something like that?!

I collected myself and got ready to offer some smooth line...

And then I noticed it.

"...zzzzz..."

While I'd been sitting there, anxious and confused, Megumin had slipped into the even breathing of sleep.

......Stupid, stupid kid!

3

"...Geez, with you and Megumin making all that noise last night, I couldn't sleep a wink!"

"Look, I apologize for the noise, but I only did it because jailbait here fell asleep in the middle of her watch. And anyway, what are you talking about? When I tried to wake you up for your shift, you didn't even budge! Darkness ended up taking your watch instead."

"I just heard that you'd done something really awful to Megumin when she fell asleep on her shift, so I thought maybe if I fell asleep—but then I was so excited about what you might do to me that I couldn't sleep..."

"Errgh... I—I can't believe what you did to me..."

True, there had been more than a little commotion the night before, but at least we'd made it safely till morning. We had a light breakfast and then walked along, arguing, with no suspicions that anything would go less than according to plan.

"Aww, crap..."

But now I stood smack in the middle of the road, staring dumbly at the huge field that spread out in front of us. There wasn't a single obstacle, meaning my Ambush skill was useless. We'd been relying on Megumin, but if we used magic in such an open space, the sound could easily attract more monsters. And the only way to Crimson Magic Village was through this field...

Even with Sense Foe active, we would be so exposed that any monsters would probably be on us before my skill could be of any use. No choice, then. This was the time to use Second Sight. I wouldn't try to use Sense Foe at all and instead just spot the monsters before they spotted me.

"Okay, I'm going in alone. You guys stay wherever you can make a quick getaway. Aqua, give me a speed boost so I can escape if I need to."

Even if a monster did get to me, Aqua's speed buff plus the Flee skill I'd learned the other day would allow me to draw the enemy off while the other three waited somewhere discreet. I took off my chest armor, gloves, and greaves, handing them to Aqua. I wanted to be as light as possible if the need arose. To reduce my weight even more, I gave her all my weapons, except my dagger.

"You look like you're set on running at the first sign of trouble," Aqua said archly. "Brave as ever."

"There's no way I could fight the monsters around here head-on," I said. "I looked at the monster info, and they all sound like serious trouble. No guarantees they'll come one at a time, either. So you're right—combat is absolutely a last resort for me."

The monster info had referred to One-Punch Bears, along with griffins, Fire Drakes, and a rogue's gallery of other creatures with very intimidating names.

Well, except for one. It was highly recognizable, and in video games and manga it was always a small fry. So if I had to meet anything, I hoped it would be that.

I got ready to set off. "All right. Follow me, but keep a good distance. Just be sure not to lose sight of me. I'll gesture if there's anything out there—then you guys run."

"Got it!" Aqua said. "You can count on me!"

"If there's one thing I've learned, it's that gestures mean nothing to you. Darkness, Megumin, you're up."

The two of them nodded.

4

The road ran through a huge field. I proceeded along it by myself, lightly armored and carefully looking around for any sign of monsters. From time to time, I looked over my shoulder to make sure the girls were still following me. All good so far. I wanted to be especially careful of any fliers. The info had mentioned griffins, but I didn't see any circling shadows.

We had seen the shapes of several huge monsters in the distance, but we had successfully avoided them. All good. We just needed to get across the field and link back up.

And then...

A human shape stood smack in the middle of the field. Whoever it was didn't seem to have noticed me yet, but I also couldn't think of any reason for someone to be standing in the middle of this field. That meant it was probably a monster.

I managed to pick out what it was while I was still at a distance. It was the only thing that seemed out of place in an area crawling with deadly enemies.

An orc.

These bipedal, pigheaded creatures were very fertile and could breed all year round. Their body type made it possible for them to breed with most other humanoids, meaning that if they captured you, life could get very unpleasant. Some people even said that if it looked like they were going to capture you, it was better to just kill yourself.

In games and such, orcs tend to rank with kobolds and goblins at the bottom of the monster totem pole. I couldn't imagine why they were listed in the monster info here. Compared to the massive foes we had been working so hard to avoid, it hardly seemed like there was a reason to bother going around this guy. True, I had only my dagger, but from what I could tell, the other guy didn't have any weapon at all. Plus, I could absorb his HP with Drain Touch—and anyway, there was only one.

I decided to get close and take him out with a single blow from my dagger. I started advancing toward the silhouette, which seemed quite a ways away. I walked boldly, making no effort to hide myself. Then again, in this huge open field, there was nowhere to hide in the first place.

When I had gotten a good deal closer, the monster must have noticed me, because he started approaching me. I reflexively tightened my grip on my dagger. Then I heard something behind me.

"…zu…ma…! Kazu…!!"

I turned around to see what was going on and spotted Aqua and the others shouting something at me. I couldn't quite tell from this distance, but Aqua and Megumin seemed to be making some kind of gesture. It took me a moment, but eventually I figured out what they were trying to say.

Run!

But I faced front again. It was just one orc.

The orc was pretty close now, and staring straight at me.

Disturbed by my companions' actions, I muttered, "*Create Earth!*" in a quiet voice, hiding some dust in my left hand so I could blind the orc if need be. When I glanced back, I saw Aqua and Megumin gesturing more frantically than ever. *Run! Run!*

If anything, it's you ladies who ought to be running, I wanted to tell them. An orc was more likely to go after women than after a man like me. But then again, since I was going to drop the thing right here, I guess it didn't really matter whether they ran or not.

I turned back to the orc. It was close enough that we could see each other's faces now, and it seemed more human than I'd pictured an orc looking. It had the ears and snout of a pig, but the structure of its face wasn't so different from anyone else's. And it had actual clothes on—probably stolen from some unfortunate traveler. The most surprising thing, though, was that it had a head of hair. Messy hair, yes, but there it was. Despite the green skin, it could easily be mistaken for a human at first glance.

"Hello! I say, you manly man! Want to have a little fun with me?"

Apparently, it was a female, because the words that came fluently out of its mouth were high-pitched.

…Gosh. This really was not at all the way I imagined orcs. I didn't even know they *had* females. I mean, sure, they were supposed to be super fertile, but I had heard they could breed with other races…

I glanced at her again. The form was humanoid, but that was definitely a monster. I felt kind of bad for her—she had gone out of her way to make me an offer—but I was not broad-minded enough to see her as a potential partner. As nonchalantly as I could, I said, "I'd rather not."

And there it was. The first time in my life a woman had propositioned me, and I'd turned her down.

The orc showed no change of expression, despite my refusal. "Oh no? That's a shame. I do so prefer when they're willing." Then she grinned, baring her teeth. Besides the messy hair, she had yellow teeth and was distinctly rotund. Snout or no snout, I couldn't say I would have been interested.

Also, what was that about being willing?

"Listen," I said, "it seems like you can talk, so let me make *you* an offer. I'd like to get through here. If you let me by, I'll share some of my rations with you... What do you say?"

Food could be a powerful motivator... Such was my naive hope, anyway. Come to think of it, what *was* that dried meat we had? It wasn't pork, was it? I'd hate to make her commit cannibalism.

As I stood mulling this over, the orc's mouth began to water. *Wow. I guess food was a good move.*

...So what she said next pulled that rug out from under me.

"I don't care about that. This area belongs to us lovely orcs. And when it comes to men in our territory, there's no such thing as the one that got away... Aren't you interesting? You don't look like much at first glance, but I feel a potent survival drive from you. I have a good nose for these things. I bet you and I could have very strong children... Sure you don't want to have a little fun?"

............*Um.*

It finally started to sink in that she wasn't kidding. Nearing the end of my rope, I looked back at my party again. Two of them were continuing to make the *run* gesture. Only Darkness, apparently oblivious to the situation, seemed to be wondering whether to join me in battle.

My backward glance gave away my companions to the orc.

"Oh, friends of yours? ...All females? I'll pretend I didn't see them. As for you... Let's see. Three days. Spend three days at our village, won't you? Tee-hee-hee! It'll be like having your own little harem. We'll give you a taste of heaven on earth. Although to be fair, most of the men we catch end up tasting heaven in the afterlife, too!"

Looking at the leering orc, I felt an instinctive terror and chanted my magic.

"*Wind Breath*!"

"Grah?!"

The wind magic carried my handful of dust straight into the orc's eyes. Blinded, she howled and bent over double. I rushed up and reached out—not with my dagger but with my bare hand, grabbing the orc.

5

I used Drain Touch to absorb the orc's HP to within an inch of her life but didn't kill her. Seeing how I'd been up all night, it was the perfect time for a little vitality boost. The orc had said something about a village, though. I was afraid that if I finished her off, her friends might come looking for me. So I left her alive. But after a few minutes of walking along, I sensed something behind me. I turned around to see Aqua and the others rushing up toward me.

"...What's the deal? If you get this close to me, then I'm not going ahead anymore, am I? Keep back a little!"

"What are you talking about, Kazuma?! You felled an orc! And this whole field is their territory! They're going to be after you until you can escape!" Megumin said, agitated.

...Doesn't she get it yet?

"If they're after me, that's a *good* thing. Remember how I took off all my armor and weapons? It was so I could play the bait. I don't want to see orcs capture you guys and, you know...do all that awful stuff orcs do to their captives."

Orcs were renowned for their sexual appetites. If my party members fell into their hands...well, I didn't even want to think about it.

"Now I remember," Aqua said. "You don't know the first thing about this world, do you, Kazuma? I'd almost forgotten what a pathetically uninformed moron you are. Well, looks like it's up to me to fill you iiirrggh!"

I grabbed Aqua's cheek before her tone could get any higher or mightier and looked to Megumin to clue me in.

"...Kazuma, listen carefully. There are no male orcs in this world."

"Say *what*?!" That wasn't me. That was Darkness, who apparently found this to be a tragedy.

"All the male orcs went extinct ages ago," Megumin went on. "Male infants are born from time to time, but they die of physical exhaustion at the hands of the females long before they reach adulthood. So there are no pure-blooded orcs left—they've crossbred with every species they can get their hands on, taking the best genes from each. You can hardly call them orcs anymore. Anytime a male—of any species—wanders into their territory, they drag him back to their village and do the most unspeakable things to him. They are men's natural enemies! ...And, Kazuma, you..." She seemed to have trouble getting out the last part of her explanation.

"W-wait just a second, orcs are supposed to be the natural enemies of female knights!" our Crusader piped up. "What happened to those lustful orc men who go after women...?!"

"All gone." Then Megumin resumed her previous thought. "Kazuma, you brought down an orc female. The orcs want the best men with the strongest genes. You succeeded in stopping one of them, which will only prove to them that they can't afford to let you go... Look. Just like that." Ignoring the stricken Darkness, Megumin pointed into the distance.

A crowd of orc females was lined up together, with the one whose HP I had drained at the very front. I knew Megumin said orcs had the best genes from every creature, but surely she couldn't have recovered so quickly?

Not all the orcs had pig ears. Some of them had cat ears or dog ears, manifest proof of the orcs' interbreeding.

"You really are a catch!" cried the one I had KO'd. "To knock *me* senseless! I'm in love now! ...And I'm keeping you! I hope you'll come quietly—I'm going to have your babies for sure!"

Now, *that* made my hair stand on end. And no sooner had she spoken than the whole horde of them charged at me!

"Huh?! Hey! Wait just a— Eeeyaaaaaahhh!"

O God! I apologize from the depths of my being! Please, I beg of you, forgive me!

Why is this happening to me? Have I offended the true God somehow? Was it that weird-shaped rock Aqua liked so much that I threw away? I didn't mean it, God, I swear! She'll bring home the strangest junk if I let her!

Or is this because I washed her divine feather mantle together with my underwear? I didn't mean it, God, I swear! I only did it because stains come out so easily when you wash things with heavenly garments!

I'm sorry! From the bottom of my heart!

So... Please, God—!

"I want a son first! Sixty-four sons and forty-four daughters! And then we can live in a little white house by the sea, and you and I can do it every day!"

Give me a break! Fine… I have to do them in before they do me!

Without another moment of hesitation, I thrust with my dagger, but the orcs, with all their excellent genes, dodged it without breaking a sweat…!

"Wonderful! This won't take a moment. Just lie still and close your eyes…!"

They easily knocked the dagger from my hands and shoved me to the ground.

I was a fool. I was a fool to think orcs couldn't be as powerful as everything else around here!

"Help meeee! Megumin, do the usual! Take them all out at once!"

"If I use Explosion while we're standing this close, it will catch us as well! Darkness! Stop moping already and do something to help Kazuma…!"

"We can talk!" I exclaimed desperately as an orc reached out for me. "Let's talk!"

"Pillow talk? Happily! Well, spill it. Tell me about all your *embarrassing* habits! *Pant! Pant! Pant! Pant!*"

Breathing heavily, the orc tore at my jacket.

Drain Touch!

I just needed to use my skill to render the creature powerless. I reached out from under where the orc had straddled me, but she merely batted my hand aside and seized my wrist. For good measure, she gave my palm a wet lick. As if my hair wasn't standing up already.

Seriously, God! What do I have to do for you to forgive me?!

In a voice nearing a scream, I made a last-ditch appeal…!

"W-wait a second! Stooop! Your name! I don't even know your name or how old you are! This might be my first time, and if I'm going to lose my virginity to you, I think—I think we should at least be introduced! My name is Kazuma Satou!"

"I'm Swatinaze, just turned sweet sixteen! Now I'll get introduced—to your *whole* body! Let me meet your little man!"

"He's very shy! In fact, I think we've learned plenty about each other for today! So let's just stop n— Aaaahhh! Aqua! Aquaaa! Help meeee!"

"Kazuma, nooo!"

I was screaming like a little girl, and Aqua was just plain screaming, when—

"*Bottomless Swamp!*"

I knew that voice. A series of shouts followed it. Still collapsed on the ground, I turned my head toward the shout and saw the orcs mired in a giant swamp. And behind them...

"Yunyun! It's you! Waaaaah!"

At the sight of the Crimson Magic Clan girl, I started sobbing with relief.

"?!" The orc who had mounted me gulped. She seemed to be confused by the swamp that had suddenly appeared and swallowed her friends. She got off me, watching Yunyun closely.

I fled, by which I mean crawled, toward Yunyun, my face still wet with tears.

"Yunyun! Yunyun! Thank youuuuu!" I wept, clinging to her.

"Eep...! Mr. K-Kazuma?! It's all right, you're safe now, so please don't cry... Ooh... You're...going to get snot all over my...precious...robe..."

Yunyun seemed to feel a little awkward, but I couldn't quite catch what she was saying. The orc never took her eyes off the wizard, except for a glance at her companions in the swamp. She seemed to want to help them but wasn't able to make a move with Yunyun there.

Aqua came over near where I was curled up on the ground. "I'm so glad you're safe, Kazuma... K-Kazuma?! What are you doing?"

I clung to her ankles, weeping afresh. I had never been so terrified in all my life, not even when facing down the generals of the Demon King.

"Okay, it's all right, shh. It must have been very scary, but you're all right now. We'll protect you," Aqua said, patting my head. I was kind of embarrassed to admit that she was actually making me feel better.

I glanced at the orc and saw Yunyun flare her cape dramatically (if with a hint of embarrassment). She thrust out her wand and declared:

"**My name is Yunyun, Arch-wizard and wielder of advanced magic! One of the top five wizards of the Crimson Magic Clan, and she who shall be its chief…!** You orcs have made a settlement near our village. Because we are good neighbors, I will let you go this one time. Now take your friends and be gone!"

At this, the orc tore a strip from her clothes and used it as a rope to rescue her drowning companions.

"Kazuma," Yunyun called, "now's our chance. Let's go!"

6

When we had gotten out of the orcs' field and into a forest, we decided to take a little breather.

"With you along, Yunyun, none of these monsters are scary at all! We can walk all over them!" That was Aqua, just begging to trip a flag.

But I did understand how she felt. Yunyun and her advanced magic were definitely heartening.

For my part, I hadn't left Aqua's side since earlier. Somehow it made me feel better, being with someone I'd known for so long. My behavior seemed to perplex her, but for once she didn't complain. I was thankful that she let me hang around her.

Really, really thankful.

It seemed like my experience with the orcs had pretty well traumatized me. I changed my ripped clothing and reequipped the items I had handed to the others. Then I turned toward my savior.

"Yunyun, thank you again. Really, you can't imagine how grateful I am. For the rest of my life, when someone asks me, 'Who's your hero?' I'll say 'Yunyun' without missing a beat. That's how grateful I am."

"A-all right, already! It's starting to sound like you're making fun of me…," Yunyun said, clearly as embarrassed as she could possibly get.

I hadn't loosened my grip on Aqua's feather mantle the whole time I spoke.

"By the way," Yunyun went on, "what's everyone doing here, anyway? Megumin, did you finally decide you were worried about the village?"

"Y-yes! My little sister! I got very worried about her. She is so quick to do very dumb things."

"Oh—oh yeah. She loves to fight so much, even though she can't use magic."

Yunyun seemed to swallow this hook, line, and sinker. The rest of us, however, all had huge smirks on our faces.

"Wh-why is everyone looking at me like that?!" Megumin said, angrily turning her back on us.

I cradled a mug of coffee in my hands, sipping slowly. Bit by bit, it helped heal my heart, which had been so badly wounded by my encounter with the orcs. Wrapped in my cloak, I stared at each of my companions.

"...All four of you have such lovely faces!"

In the woods lining the road, the others froze at the sound of my voice.

"Wh-what's going on?" Aqua said. "Kazuma is always saying and doing weird stuff, but today he seems worse than usual!"

"S-stay calm," Darkness answered. "He's planning something; I know it. He loves to build you up just to bring you down. Don't act happy, or you'll be walking right into his trap!"

Sheesh. Rude.

Megumin still had her back to us, but she glanced over her shoulder at me, working her mouth as if to say that she agreed with Darkness. And Yunyun just seemed startled, her cheeks red.

I had never felt more relieved than now, after escaping those orcs. I looked at my four traveling companions and took another breath.

"You all really are very beautiful, aren't you?"

"*What* is he doing?!" Aqua said. "Seriously, what? He's acting super weird!"

"I told you, Aqua, stay calm. Start by casting healing magic on him!"

Darkness and Aqua were on the verge of panic, and Megumin looked like she was keeping her guard up. Way, way up.

I looked at Yunyun, beet-red and staring at the ground, and relished the joy of having escaped the orcs.

7

"Megumin, when we were in school, you were always the best in Magic Studies and had the most MP. The villagers wouldn't stop talking about how gifted you were. Everyone expected so much of you... I hate to think what will happen when they find out you became a failure of a wizard who can only use explosive magic..."

"Hey, I shall have you cease calling me a failure of a wizard! In terms of sheer magical power, I am undoubtedly first among the Crimson Magic Clan. I am not spouting falsehoods! I shall not have you speak ill of the explosive magic to which I have dedicated nearly my entire life."

We had broken camp and set off down the road again.

"But what good is it?! You can't use it in a dungeon, because the whole place might come crashing down on your head. It's great at long distances, but you can't use it when the enemy gets close, because you might blow yourself up along with all your friends. It uses an unsustainable amount of MP—even as a high-level wizard, you can only do it once. And the one thing it has going for it, the power, is always going to be overkill! Nobody takes Explosion because it just eats up all your skill points, and for what? A gimmick!"

Yunyun and Megumin had been at it for a while. Apparently, Megumin hadn't actually told anyone in the village that she could use only Explosion. Yunyun was trying to do damage control, but she wasn't having much success...

Megumin turned to face her squarely. "...Oh, you have done it now, Yunyun! You have said something unforgivable. Something worse than insulting my very name!"

"I-is that how it is? Okay, you and me, right here and now. I'm done losing to you, Megumin!" Yunyun backed away from Megumin, keeping one eye on the other wizard. Megumin took a single look at her, and...!

"Kazuma. Let me tell you all of Yunyun's dirty secrets. Did you know that we Crimson Magic Clan members are born with a tattoo on our bodies? Its exact location varies from person to person, but Yunyun's, believe it or not, is on her—"

"Stop it! How can you say that to Mr. Kazuma?! Never mind that—how do you know where my tattoo is?! You can't use your Explosion here, Megumin. And with no magic, I won't have any trouble getting you good!" Almost in tears, Yunyun charged at Megumin, but Megumin easily dodged her.

"Aqua, buff me! I shall show her what it means to be gotten good!"

"Why—why, you! You're a cheater, Megumin! You always were!"

That's when it happened.

Perhaps drawn by the sound of the girls fighting, an unpleasantly screechy voice came through the trees.

"Hey, over here! I knew I heard people this way!"

"It looks like the enemy's heard us!" Darkness hissed, crouching down. "Both of you be quiet now!"

"It is Yunyun's fault! She keeps shouting! She gets angry so easily."

"You're one to talk, Megumin! You always just go ahead and do whatever you want without ever thinking about the consequences! Chomusuke hasn't even been trying to come out from under your hat for I don't know how long!"

"What was that?!"

"Will both of you please shut up?! If you keep shouting, they'll find us! Tell them, Kazuma!"

As Megumin and Yunyun continued their argument, Darkness placed a hand on each of their heads and shoved them into the bushes. They stopped arguing but kept making angry eye movements and gestures at each other. I exclaimed:

* * *

"That doesn't matter right now! You have to tell me where Yunyun's tattoo is!"

"They're here; I found them! They're hiding over here!"
"You impossible man! You impossible, impossible man!"

8

"I found two Crimson Magic Clan members! The others look like human adventurers. Hey, over here! Get over here! Two little Crimson Magic kids! This is our chance! What a haul!"

The monster was wearing armor. It had pointed ears, reddish-brown skin, and it was slim rather than muscular. A demon. A single horn grew from its forehead, and its glittering eyes were fixed firmly on Megumin and Yunyun.

Off to its side, Aqua and Darkness stood up from where they'd been hidden in the bushes, and...!

"Huh? Are you pretending to be a low-level demon or something? You look ridiculous! What are you, a washout who couldn't even make the bottom of the demon ranks? Whatever! Exorcism magic doesn't even work on monsters as pitiful as you. Aren't you lucky to be such a loser! I don't have time to act like I care about you. Come back when you make full demon. I'll pretend I didn't see you here, so get. Get!"

I couldn't tell if she was taunting it or trying to intimidate it. Either way, the demon ground its teeth at her. Darkness wordlessly stepped forward, drawing her great sword.

Given that this creature was wearing armor, it must have been part of the army of the Demon King, currently at war with the Crimson Magic Clan. We were getting close to the village, so it wasn't surprising that we would run into the foot soldiers. This one was clutching a short spear in hand and staring at us in fury, red face growing even redder.

And then a crowd of similar creatures appeared behind it. They all carried different items, but they were clearly armed. Monster soldiers.

Hang on—this isn't good. I mean, there were five of us and…a *lot* of them!

"You think you're letting me go, huh, priest? …You've got two little Crimson Magic kids right there—ain't no way we're missing out on this! Chop 'em up, boys!"

There had to be at least twenty monsters backing him up. But Yunyun took a step forward…

"*Light of Saber*!!"

As she yelled, she made a diagonal slicing motion through the air with her hand. A ray of light followed the motion. As it passed through the demons, they suddenly found parts of their bodies missing or they just collapsed right to the ground.

The demon we had been speaking to wasn't taking this well. "S-surround them! Circle up! They can't stop all of us at once! Everybody dogpile and get that Crimson Magic wench first!"

Darkness stepped between Yunyun and the demons who were trying to surround her to fend them off. Aqua was busy casting buffs on our Crusader.

"You have some nerve, Yunyun, referring to my magic as a gimmick! It's been a long time since I got to show you just how powerful a gimmick can be!"

"What? Stop! You're not going to—?!"

"*Explosion*!!"

Completely ignoring the frantic Yunyun, Megumin let loose on the soldiers who were watching from a distance, catching a huge number of them in a titanic blast.

The other demons goggled as they got a close-up view of her power, trees pulled by the roots and flung around. When the dust had settled, all that was left was a massive crater.

"Did you see my most profound magical technique?! Do you still have the gall to call it a mere gimmick? What do you think, Kazuma? How many points for that explosion?!"

"Minus ninety! How stupid can you be, just up and using your magic like that?! There are still bad guys here! I can't pick you up and run away!"

"M-Mr. Kazuma," Yunyun said, "while you were talking, a bunch of new enemies noticed the noise and came over here!"

Despite what I'd said, I struggled to heave Megumin off the ground.

For some reason, Aqua was out front now, looking more confident than she had any right to. "What are you doing?! You actually think you can fight them?!" I shouted, using Drain Touch to transfer some MP to Megumin.

She cocked her head at me. At first I thought she was giving me a questioning look, but then I realized she just wanted to crack her neck.

She kicked the ground a few times, took a little bow, and made a fist. "Heh-heh! You know who I am. Surely, you don't think healing magic is all I'm good for? I am the great Aqua! All my stats are maxed out! What's a few low-level demons? I could take on that whole crowd with one hand tied behind my back. Just watch—I do have my goddess-like moments!"

... *This is bad.*

It was already all too obvious to me what was going to happen. I increased my MP transfer to Megumin, giving her my shoulder to lean on and standing her up.

I looked at the Demon King's soldiers. The explosion had given them a fright, but they had pulled themselves together and were tightening their circle. At least we had Yunyun on our side, but there were just too many of them. We didn't even know how many of them there were, and I didn't know how well I could run with the magic-less Megumin in tow.

"Aqua, we're getting out of here! Don't just stand there striking stupid poses; let's go!"

She was standing there, striking a variety of stupid poses in the direction of the enemy. I turned around, about to order a general retreat, when I heard Aqua mutter, "...Oh."

I turned back around. In the distance, I could see even more agents of the Demon King heading our way at breakneck speed. They weren't even carrying their weapons—they had thrown them aside so as to reach us faster.

......?!

I was just wondering who they could possibly be when...

...suddenly, four people in black robes appeared out of thin air.

No, not all of them wore robes. Two were in something like black motorcycle outfits. Some of them held short staves, and some had no weapon at all. There might have been more people hidden nearby, but I could see only the four of them. And while their weapons and clothes were mismatched, there was one thing they all had in common: their red eyes.

All four of the black-clad newcomers had deep crimson eyes, just like Megumin and Yunyun. They were from the Crimson Magic Clan.

They must have been hiding themselves with magic—that was how they'd seemed to appear from nothing. And the Demon King soldiers who were headed our way at such a fearsome pace—it wasn't that they had noticed us and were coming to attack; they had realized the Crimson Magic people were there before the rest of us had and were trying to beat feet.

As if to prove me right, the enemy screeched to a halt, looking in confusion first at the pursuing Crimson Magic Clanners, then at the four of us. They must have decided we would be easier to handle, because they turned toward us and prepared to charge...!

But then...

"May your flesh vanish without a trace—in the dark fire born from the abyss of my heart!"

"Argh! It's no use; I can't hold back anymore! You shall be the sacrifices that calm the tumult of destruction within me!"

"Now sleep forever...fast in the embrace of my ice...!"

"Go into the next life. I shall not forget you… I shall carve you into the memories of my soul forevermore…!"

Those were chants of…well, not magic. They had to be catch-phrases or something. The Crimson Magic wizards must have had buffs on their physical abilities, because they caught up with the soldiers in no time. Then they all began the exact same chant. One of the Demon King's soldiers stuck out a hand…!

"P-please— Wait— Wait just a—!"

He tried to say something, but the Crimson Magic Clan people had already finished their incantation.

"*Light of Saber!*"

"*Light of Saber!*"

"*Saber!*" "*Saber!!*"

As they called out, their knife hands began to glow. They carved through the air, then thrust at the Demon King's minions. And in the space of a moment…

All that was left on the field was a pile of bits.

Holy crap! These Crimson Magic Clanners are scary as hell!

So scary that the Demon King's soldiers, who had vastly outnumbered them, went running for their lives. So scary that I was even a little afraid to make a smarmy remark about how all that dark-fire and icy-embrace stuff ended up seeming kind of irrelevant.

Then one of the Crimson Magic Clan people looked at me. It was the man who had mentioned flesh vanishing without a trace. "We followed the Demon King's strike team here when we heard the rumbling from that explosion," he said. "But to think we would find you, Megumin and Yunyun! What are you doing here?" His tone was weirdly conversational.

Megumin responded in kind, getting unsteadily to her feet. "If it is not Bukkororii, the cobbler's son. It's been a long time. We heard the village was in trouble and came rushing back."

"Trouble?" Bukkororii said, giving Megumin a puzzled look.

…Huh?

I noticed the other Crimson Magic Clan people were looking at me with interest. Then the man called Bukkororii said, "Megumin, are these your adventuring companions?"

Megumin nodded, looking more than a little pleased. This brought a stern frown to Bukkororii's face, and he gave a dramatic flourish of his robe.

"My name is Bukkororii! First among the cobblers' sons of the Crimson Magic Clan! Arch-wizard and wielder of advanced magic...!"

Well, that self-introduction certainly came out of left field.

In the old days, this might have been where I would have tuned out, but my experience with Megumin and Yunyun had given me a bit of tolerance for these things.

"A pleasure to meet you," I replied, striking a genial tone somewhat like Bukkororii's. "My name is Kazuma Satou. Learner of many skills in Axel Town and occasional opponent of the Demon King's generals."

""""Oooooh!"""""

All four of the Crimson Magic Clan wizards seemed duly impressed.

"Wonderful, absolutely wonderful!" Bukkororii exclaimed. "Most people have the strangest reactions when they hear our Crimson Magic names, but you...! To think that an outsider should answer us in kind!" The others nodded emphatically.

"...Kazuma, you seem to get along awfully well with Bukkororii and the others. I wish you had responded so readily when I introduced myself!" There was something strange in Megumin's voice, and I wasn't sure how I should respond. Normally, I might think it was a hint of jealousy, or maybe nervous excitement. But given that I was talking to an older guy, I couldn't imagine what she was jealous of.

...But Crimson Magic Clan people could be sensitive. Maybe I had touched a nerve.

What was going on? She wasn't jealous, but I didn't think she was especially happy, either. It was hardly as if we were about to break out into a romantic comedy or something.

As I was still trying to puzzle this out...

"My name is Aqua! Venerated being and she who shall finally destroy the Demon King! And my true identity is the goddess of water!"

...Aqua suddenly launched into a totally uninvited self-introduction. She seemed to have taken to Crimson Magic Clan ways very quickly.

""""""Oh, really? Good for you."""""""

"Hey, what gives? Why does everyone always do this to me?!"

Ignoring Aqua and her whining, the Crimson Magic Clan people looked expectantly at Darkness. She said falteringly:

"M-my name is L-Lalatina...F-Ford...Dusti...ne...ss...of Axel Town, and... Nnngh..."

Despite her obvious desire to please, being the center of attention slowly sapped her ability to speak.

Don't hurt yourself.

As Darkness stood with tears of embarrassment beading in her eyes, turning red and muttering to herself, Bukkororii smiled widely and began to chant a spell in a loud voice.

"Lovely friends you have, Megumin," he said. "We're still a ways from the village. Come, outsiders, we will guide you. Let's go by Teleport!" And then he intoned the spell.

I suddenly found my vision warping and dizziness assailing me as the scenery changed in the blink of an eye.

We found ourselves in a tiny hamlet, the very definition of *idyllic*. As the rest of us took it in, dumbstruck, Bukkororii gave us another broad grin.

"Welcome, outsiders, to Crimson Magic Village. And to Megumin and Yunyun—welcome home!"

Chapter 3

May We Get Some R&R in This Pitiful Village!

1

"We'll get back to our patrol, then," Bukkororii said, edging away from us. He and the other three clustered together, and after he intoned a brief bit of magic—

"See you later!"

—all four of them vanished from sight.

Awesome! Now those are some real wizards. They must have teleported straight back to the battlefield...!

"They are so cool," I said admiringly, still not taking my eyes off the place where they had disappeared. "They're like an elite combat brigade or something."

"You think so? I'm sure they're very happy to hear that," Megumin said, still leaning on my shoulder.

"What do you mean, they *are* very happy? They've already teleported away, right?"

But Yunyun answered, "They disappeared using magic that bends light. Teleport takes a lot of MP. If they used it after every battle, they wouldn't have enough magic to last a whole day. I'm pretty sure they just disappeared like that because they wanted to make a dramatic exi— Eyow!"

Suddenly a pebble came flying from where the other wizards had been standing, bopping Yunyun on the head. Sort of a warning to keep her mouth shut.

...So they *were* there.

"Incidentally, light-bending magic creates a field a few yards in diameter around a specific person or object, making it invisible to everyone outside of it. But if you get close enough, you can still see it," Megumin said blandly.

This prompted Aqua to take a few quiet steps forward.

"...!"

There was a tiny gasp of distress and the noise of something scuttling backward. Aqua froze in her tracks, staring intently but not moving...

"............"

"............"

...until she suddenly jumped forward.

""""""?!""""""

At the same moment, I could hear several people scrambling away.

Oh, quit it already...

I turned away from Aqua, who was merrily chasing the invisible thing around, and the rest of us headed into the village. For starters, we would go to Yunyun's house and see if we could figure out what was going on.

Aqua finally caught up with us, having apparently tired of the chase.

"Hey, those people are something, huh?" she said. "Even I couldn't catch them!"

So they'd gotten away from Aqua, who did have strong stats in everything except Intelligence and Luck. Exactly how they had managed to escape was somewhat ambiguous, but they must have been a true special-strike team. Elites among the Crimson Magic villagers, no doubt.

"They probably doped themselves up with physical buffs so they could run away. I can't imagine the NEET brigade has all that much stamina, lolling about like they do every day." ...And thus Megumin stuck a pin in my admiring fantasies.

"...What do you mean, the NEET brigade? Aren't they a special guerrilla strike force, doing battle with the Demon King's army?" I asked. "They even said they were going back on patrol."

"Those people never managed to get jobs, so they have plenty of time on their hands. If they went to some other town to become adventurers, they would probably find everybody wanted to party up with them, but they just want to stay in the village, never cutting the apron strings. They decided to call themselves a strike force and wander the village because they didn't want everyone to notice that they were just sitting around all day."

Megumin gave me an answer, but I thought I would have been happier not knowing it.

And anyway, so what? Apparently, even the NEETs around here could kick some serious butt.

"Everyone in the Crimson Magic Clan learns advanced magic when they grow up," Yunyun said, reading my mind. "Every single person in the village belongs to the Arch-wizard class. After learning advanced magic, they pick up as many different spells as their skill points allow. At least, that's what they normally do..."

Megumin avoided looking at Yunyun under the guise of taking in the nostalgic sights of her hometown. Crimson Magic Village was about the size of a small farming settlement. None of the various clan members I saw looked the least bit concerned about anything; in fact, some of them were yawning openly. Maybe the spring weather was getting to them.

Really, this didn't look like a place at war with the Demon King at all...

Darkness spoke up. "...Mm. This is quite a griffin statue. Did a famous sculptor carve it?" She was patting a stone sculpture near the entrance to the village. I could see what she meant: The griffin was so realistic, it looked like it might swoop down and grab one of us in its talons at any moment...

"That is a griffin that wandered into the village and was turned to stone by petrification magic," Megumin said. "It looks rather cool, so we decided to leave it there as a tourist attraction. These days, people mostly use it as a landmark when they're trying to meet up."

Wh-what a ridiculous tourist attraction.

After Megumin's explanation, Aqua was patting the statue with great interest, muttering something to herself.

"Hey, you," I said. "What's that spell you're using?"

"Just some magic to reverse status effects. I want to see a real live griffin!"

The four of us dragged Aqua away and headed for Yunyun's place to find out just what was going on.

2

Her home was a big house in the middle of the village. We were at a table with sofas on either side, where a middle-aged man sat furrowing his brow. This was the sitting room of the chief of the Crimson Magic Clan, and that was the chief himself in front of us—that is to say, Yunyun's father.

"Aww, that? That was just a letter to let my daughter know what was going on. I got a bit carried away was all. My Crimson Magic Clan blood just won't let me write a normal letter…"

"Sir, you're not making any sense," I said pointedly. Beside me, Yunyun's mouth was hanging open.

"…What? D-Dad? Not that I'm not happy you're safe and all, but could you go over that again? Your letter began, '**By the time this letter reaches you, I will be dead**'…"

"Why, that's the way members of the Crimson Magic Clan have always opened their letters. Didn't they teach you in school? …Ah, you and Megumin both had such good grades; you graduated early, didn't you?"

"…And the part about not being able to destroy the Demon King's base?"

"Oh yes, they put up a pretty impressive encampment. No one can agree on whether to tear it down or leave it there as a new tourist attraction."

"Hey, Yunyun. Mind if I sock your dad one?"

"Be my guest."

"Yunyun?!"

Darkness gave Yunyun's appalled father a quizzical look. "...Hmm? Just a moment. You said the Demon King's army really did establish a base, right? So were you telling the truth about one of his generals being here, too?"

"Oh yes, one who's strong against magic, just like I wrote in my letter. She'll be around soon. Wanna have a look?"

Just as the chief was offering us his easygoing invitation...

"Alert! The Demon King's forces are approaching. Alert! The Demon King's forces are approaching! All who are able, please assemble near the griffin statue. The enemy appears to number roughly a thousand."

""A th—?!""

Darkness and I both reacted with shock, but the three Crimson Magic Clanners looked as if this was nothing special. Maybe they hadn't heard the part about there being *a thousand* enemies out there. This whole village was home to at most three hundred, by my reckoning. More than triple that number of the Demon King's soldiers was on their way, and these guys were acting like it was no big deal.

Aqua, demonstrating an unusual maturity as she sipped the tea that had been brought out, said suddenly, "A thousand of the Demon King's minions, huh? Looks like it might finally be time to show the true power of a goddess." This village seemed to be having a really weird effect on her.

I'm begging you, please, please don't do anything else stupid...

Darkness sat frozen. Megumin said calmly to her, "There is no need to panic. This is Crimson Magic Village, and everyone here is a powerful wizard. Would you like to see?"

3

...It was really pretty amazing.

"Yargh! Yaaaaarrrgh!"

"Lady Sylvia! Milady! You must escape! Even if none of us makes it, you alone must..."

"Curses! Curse it all! We can't even get close enough to counterattack!"

"I told you we shouldn't attack Crimson Magic Village! I told you I didn't want to go!"

Before we even reached the village gate, the Demon King's forces were already routing. Barely fifty Crimson mages stood against more than a thousand foes.

And as for those fifty wizards…

"*Lightning Strike!*"

"*Energy Ignition!*"

"*Freeze Gust!!*"

"*Cursed Lightning!!!*"

"Geez… I've got to admit, I'm actually impressed."

They were unleashing a merciless barrage of magic against the vanguard of the Demon King's army.

This hardly qualified as a battle. It was a complete and utter trouncing. I expected lightning to fall on the enemy troops, but then a dozen of the demons were simply incinerated, totally out of the blue. White mist surrounded another group. I thought they would be turned to ice, but forks of black lightning pierced them, leaving holes in their chests.

…Then the sea of enemy troops parted, and from the center emerged a beautiful woman in a long dress.

"Troops! I will be your wall, so stay behind me! It'll take time before they can use their advanced magic again—that's our chance!"

Who knew the Demon King had such a hot general? She looked like nothing more than a slim human woman; her dress had a delightfully low neckline. A blue earring sparkled in her right ear, strikingly clean and pure in contrast to her flashy dress.

A group of men and women came forward to confront the general. I recognized one of the men. It was Bukkororii, who had teleported us earlier. His red eyes flashed, and he thrust out his hands. From long acquaintance with Megumin, I knew that when a Crimson Magic Clan member's eyes got redder, it meant they were getting really worked up…

"*Tornado*!!"

And it meant they were getting ready to pour a whole bunch of MP into one giant spell.

Bukkororii's incantation summoned a massive whirlwind right in the middle of the Demon King's soldiers, flinging a bunch of them helplessly into the air. The fall would probably be fatal.

The gorgeous girl next to Bukkororii held out her left hand, her eyes flashing as well. She had a weapon in her right hand, unusual for a member of the Crimson Magic Clan. I looked closer and found that it was a wooden sword carved in the shape of a dragon. Maybe it was a magical weapon or something? That might explain why a member of the Crimson Magic Clan had it.

The girl extended her left hand and gave a swipe of the sword in her right.

"*Inferno*!"

A conflagration broke out, smack in the middle of the still-raging whirlwind.

4

After watching the battle, we headed back to Megumin's house. Yunyun went her own way, saying she was going to find Arue, the one who'd sent us that letter, and give her a piece of her mind.

"Phew!" I said, reflecting back on the magic display those wizards had put on. "That was something! So that's what it's like to see *real* Crimson Magic Clan members in action."

"To refer to them as *real* suggests there are *fake* Crimson Magic Clan members. I should like to know exactly who you believe to be a fake!" With Megumin leaning on my shoulder and looking like she might bite me, we arrived at a snug one-story house. Not to be rude, but I couldn't help thinking it seemed a little poorer than the average place. Megumin, looking tired—maybe because of lack of MP—went up and knocked on the front door.

A moment later, feet thumped toward us from inside. The door opened slowly...

Out peeked a girl, about primary school age, who resembled Megumin.

"Ooh, is that your little sister, Megumin? She's pretty cute," Darkness said, breaking into a smile.

"Megumin, she's like a tiny version of you! C'mere, mini-Megumin. Want some candy?" Aqua was suddenly holding some candy. I had no idea where she'd gotten it. But before the girl could react—

"Komekko, I'm home. Have you been a good girl?" Megumin spoke to the child in a gentle voice, still leaning on my shoulder.

Komekko...

Be it Komekko or Bukkororii, I had pretty much ceased to be surprised by Crimson Magic names. Maybe there was something wrong with me.

Komekko looked at Megumin and froze. She must have been overcome by the joy of seeing her sister again. Her eyes went wide, and she sucked in a deep breath. Then she shouted, "Daaaaad! Sis is back, and she brought a *guy!*"

All right, kid, time for you and me to have a talk!

5

"Look closely, now. See the upside-down cup on this table? I'm going to make it move all on its own!"

"Wow! Amazing! How do you do it? Hey, Blue-Haired Girl, how do you do it? Tell me!"

"It's magnetism!" Darkness said. "There's got to be a magnet under the table. That's how you're doing it, right, Aqua? Isn't it?"

We were in the living room at Megumin's house. Aqua was doing party tricks with a cup, and Komekko and Darkness were eating it up. I figured Darkness was probably right about the magnet. The cup Aqua was using was made of metal, after all. It would be easy enough to slip a magnet underneath the table...

As I listened to them try to figure out the secret to her trick, I glanced over thoughtlessly.

Aqua was sitting there in the middle of the living room, her hands folded neatly on her knees. She was staring intently at the mug on the table, but that was all—and it was moving.

……?!

I could barely believe my own eyes. I focused more and more on what was happening over there, when…

"Er…! Ahem!" The person in front of me cleared his throat pointedly.

Whoops, right!

I had gotten so caught up in what was going on that I had almost forgotten Megumin's father was sitting across from me on the carpet, fixing me with a baleful stare. At first glance, he looked almost normal, just a man with black hair. But his eyes were sharp, and he radiated a quiet, intimidating pressure. Until this moment, I had known nothing of him but his name: Megumin's father, Hyoizaburou.

"…I understand that you have been looking out for my daughter. For that, at least, I thank you." He gave a small nod.

Next to him sat an attractive woman, who somehow looked a bit like Megumin, with rich black hair and the first hints of wrinkles around her mouth and eyes. "Yes, thank you very much… Our daughter often mentions you in her letters, young Kazuma… I almost feel like we know you…" Megumin's mother, Yuiyui, bowed deeply.

I shot a withering look in the direction of the person who more than anyone else should have been here helping me clear this up. A bedroll had been laid out in the corner, and Megumin—having spent all her MP on the explosion earlier—was curled up on it, fast asleep.

Hyoizaburou took a long, meaningful look at Megumin, then turned to me, nonplussed.

"…And what exactly is the relationship between you and our daughter?"

It was the third time he had asked me that.

"...Sir, as I keep telling you, we're just friends."

At that, Hyoizaburou went over to the tea table where Aqua was doing her trick, with an expression of disgust.

"Grrraaaaaaahhhh!"

"Ohhhhhh! Stop, dear! Please! Please stop flipping over tables! You break them, and we don't have the money to replace them, especially this month!"

There really were a lot of very strange people in the Crimson Magic Clan.

Hyoizaburou sat sipping the tea his wife had made.

"You must excuse me. I lost control of myself because you keep mocking me with your insistence that you and my daughter are just friends."

I bit back the words I'd been about to say—*S-seriously, we're just friends*—and pulled something out of my item pouch, hoping to change the subject. It was a collection of the buns we had bought in Arcanletia on our recent hot-springs trip. Since we'd left Axel right after getting back, they were still in my bag.

"Uh, here... Just something small..." I held out the box of buns, and Hyoizaburou and his wife both grabbed it at the same time.

"...My dear wife. Young Kazuma was thoughtful enough to bring me a gift, so will you please take your hands off it?"

"Heavens, my love. A moment ago, you could barely even look at him, but he gives you a little something and suddenly you can remember his name. Stop now, you're embarrassing yourself. These will be our dinner tonight. I won't let you just eat them with your wine, understand?" Was she joking? If so, it wasn't very funny.

I fought down the urge to point out that meat buns weren't very good for dinner or drinks, when Komekko exclaimed happily, "Food?! Is that actual hard food?! Not, like, that nasty gruel we always eat? Actual stomach-filling *food*?!"

...I reached into my bag and pulled out all the preserved rations I had with me, spreading them out on the floor.

"Just something…really small…"

"Welcome to our home, dear Kazuma! Wife, bring a cup of our finest tea!"

"We only have one kind of tea, dear. But I'll bring it right out. You boys wait there."

I sat sipping the tea Yuiyui had brought. Komekko had a bun in each hand and was stuffing her face like a squirrel. As she gobbled them down, she watched me intently from her spot beside me. For a moment, she studied the food in her hands, then swallowed heavily.

"…Here. They're delicious." She held out a bun that was still whole. She never took her eyes off it, though, clearly famished.

"Komekko, sweetie, stop! Come over here; come back to us girls!"

"She's right, Komekko! That's a bad man who does nothing but play nasty pranks on your sister. Come over here before he turns on you!"

Komekko, however, ignored Aqua and Darkness, instead looking at me with a puzzled tilt of her head. I would have to give them what-for later. Komekko was an angel.

"Thank you, Komekko, but you eat it. I'm already full," I said.

"Oh, really?" was all she said before settling next to me again and wordlessly tearing back into the food. I could feel the corners of my lips pull up at the sight of her smile.

Hyoizaburou was eyeing me dangerously. "…I don't care how much food you bring me. You can't have Komekko."

"I'm not trying to take Komekko, sir! You don't have to listen to those two!"

Aqua snuck up to where Komekko was wolfing down meat buns beside me, then grabbed her in a hug and snatched her away as if to protect her from me.

…I'll get them for this, that's for damn sure.

Komekko continued eating, totally oblivious to being spirited away.

Yuiyui smiled and watched me sip tea, and at last said delicately, "Now, Kazuma, I hear you have quite a lot of debt. You seem like a very nice man, and I'm not opposed to you…but don't you think it might be better not to be with our daughter until after you've repaid everything…?"

I did the biggest spit take of my life.

"What do you mean, *be with*?! I keep telling you, we're *just friends*!" I said, choking.

Megumin's mother gave me a questioning look. "From my daughter's letters, I got the impression the two of you were quite intimate. Is that not the case…?"

"Okay, just a minute. Can I ask what exactly she wrote to you?"

As I tried to calm down, Hyoizaburou and his wife exchanged a glance. Then Yuiyui began, "Well, she wrote…"

Psst.
The next two pages reflect the original
Japanese orientation, so read backward!

...how you bathe together.

...how when she's napping on the couch, you crouch behind her and stare up her skirt.

...how, while feeding Chomusuke, you hold up a pair of underpants and say, "Listen up, these are what we want. You steal me some of these, and I'll get you some gourmet dinners."

"...and how her life is basically a constant stream of sexual harassment."

I had heard enough. I got on my knees and bowed deeply to her parents.

Hyoizaburou picked up the thread. "But she says that even so, you're an important friend whom she could never leave. Even if you are riddled with debt, an unrepentant pervert, have no real combat ability to speak of, abuse your friends every time you open your mouth, and don't know common sense from a hole in the ground, she says that if she ever took her eyes off you for one minute, you'd die. I assume that if she was willing to say all that, there must be something there..."

He sounded sincere. And while I wasn't exactly thrilled with everything I'd just heard, it did warm my heart a little to know that she considered me an important friend. We'd been through so much together—the bond between us was strong enough that we could forgive each other's faults. I didn't even mind knowing that she had been saying these things behind my back. My trust in her was still...

"After all," Yuiyui went on, "to hear her tell it, she provides all the firepower in your party—why, if she wasn't there, your group would fall apart! She's told us all about how she took out the Demon King's general Vanir and how she attacked the castle of another general every day to draw him out, then played a crucial role in his defeat."

...I guess those things aren't technically untrue.

She'd helped us get rid of Hans recently, too. I wasn't sure I'd say that we would fall apart without her, but...

"That's right! And she dealt the finishing blow to Mobile Fortress Destroyer! Ahhh, my little girl makes me so proud!" Hyoizaburou said, continuing where his wife left off. He did seem genuinely happy... And I mean, he wasn't *wrong*. But still...

Without thinking about it, I glanced over at the sleeping Megumin. She had been breathing deeply, but now she had her back to me...

Don't tell me she's awake.

I studied her suspiciously.

"She wrote so many other things about her party and her friends, too," Yuiyui said. "But if you don't mind my asking, what about all that debt? I can't help but worry about my daughter's party. I'd love to help in any way I can, but our family doesn't have much money..." She gave me an apologetic look.

"Oh, please," I said easily, "don't worry about it. I took care of that debt a long time ago. And I'm expecting a windfall about the time we get back from this trip. So really, we're fine—you don't have to worry."

Hyoizaburou pricked up his ears at this. "...Oh-ho. If I may ask, just how much of a windfall...?"

I didn't think too hard about the question—maybe because I was a little anxious being at Megumin's actual house—but replied, "About three hundred million eris, I guess."

""Three hundred million?!""

...Huh? Should I maybe have kept that to myself?

Hyoizaburou slid a little closer to me. Then he clapped his hands, a perfectly brilliant smile on his face. "Oh yes, Kazuma. Please stay here tonight! You all are friends of my daughter's, after all—how can I not extend my hospitality? Stay as long as you like—forever, in fact! As adventurers, you must not have a home of your own, right?"

"Oh yes!" Yuiyui said. "Komekko, let's you and Daddy and me camp out here in the living room tonight! You two girls can sleep in our room. Our house isn't very large, though. We just have this room and our room and the room that used to be Megumin's bedroom... It might be a little small for all of you to live in. Say, dear, weren't we just thinking about remodeling...?"

I wanted to break in before they could get any further ahead of themselves and said a bit hesitantly, "N-no, it's all right. We have, uh, our mansion back in Axel and all..."

""Mansion?!""

Did it again.

Megumin's parents were looking at me with shining eyes. I averted my gaze, hoping to find help from Aqua and Darkness...

"And now, for my next trick! I will do something amazing with this little box!"

"Oh! She's going to open it, and something's going to fly out from inside! I'm sure that's it, positive!"

"Wow! Amazing!"

Suffice to say, they weren't going to be any help.

6

It was late in the evening, but Megumin still hadn't woken up. It was understandable. In some ways she was the most adult member of our party, but she was still just fourteen. We had gone to Arcanletia, gotten back, and immediately left again, plus she had used up her MP on that explosion. As she slept...

"Meat, Mom! Real meat!"

"I'll take that! Dear, you have the bok choy—it's supposed to keep a woman looking young. And I want my wife to be beautiful her whole life through!"

"Oh, but my love, your hair's been thinning lately. You should have the seaweed salad with that meat!"

None of them seemed the least bit concerned about the return of a family member they hadn't seen in ages. They were completely focused on the food I had gone to get for them.

The main dish was hot pot. Aqua was drinking the wine we bought to accompany the meal, while Darkness seemed a bit anxious, as though this was her first time eating at a table with a whole family. I kept peeking around to make sure I was minding the local manners, but I was doing my part to demolish the food supply.

Finally Komekko sat back, her stomach full and her eyes shining. "Hey, Dad! Mom! Blue-Haired Girl is awesome! She pulled this huge Neroid out of a tiny little box!"

That got my attention. Darkness noticed me leaning in. "It was really something, Kazuma. It shouldn't have been physically possible! She pulled this huuuge Neroid out of that box, and it went leaping through the window. I keep wondering how she did it..."

At that, I turned to Aqua, who was happily drinking her wine. "...Hey. I've been wanting to ask you. Could you show me one of your party tricks? I mean, really show me?"

"Uh-uh. These aren't tricks, they're art, and you can't rush art. It has to emerge spontaneously, at a moment of intense emotion! If you really want to see what I can do, throw me a party that will put me in an artistic mood." As she spoke, she popped some peas—a snack to go with her alcohol—out of their pod with one hand, nimbly launching them toward my mouth. "Way to suck... I popped those peas right on target; the least you could do is catch them in your mouth... Eek, s-stop! You don't even drink that much wine; don't take all my peas!"

All in all, it was a pretty pleasant dinner. For the first time in a long while, I thought back to dinners with my family in Japan. The anxiousness of roughing it started to vanish, and I just relaxed and enjoyed the food.

It happened when I had just gotten out of the bath and was going back to the living room.

"Don't be stupid! Don't you love your own daughter?! What you're trying to do is like throwing a delicious-looking little lamb into a cage with a wild beast that hasn't eaten in a week!"

I had been the last one in the bath, and now I heard Darkness hollering something in the living room. I peeked in, wondering what all the fuss was about. There was Hyoizaburou, sawing logs. I was sure he'd been awake when I went to take my bath. He was pretty quick falling asleep. I didn't see Aqua anywhere. She must have already gone to her room.

"Now, now, they were already living in the same house together. Were there never any...mistakes? Then there's no problem! Our daughter is already of marriageable age, and Kazuma is a discerning man. If something happened between them, surely it would be because they both wanted it? And as parents, how could we object?"

Apparently, Darkness was pushing back against my sleeping in the same room with Megumin. Personally, I didn't care where I slept. Megumin's mom had a sly smile on her face.

"...If you don't mind my asking, Miss Darkness, why *are* you so against this arrangement? Is it not to your liking for Kazuma and my daughter to sleep together?"

Even I wasn't thrilled with the way she'd put that...

"What?! It almost sounds as though you think I'm jealous or something! That makes me extremely uncomfortable, and I really wish you would stop..."

...*Huh?*

"O-oh, I'm sorry. My mistake. But it would be such trouble to move my daughter to another room. *Someone* has to sleep in the same room as Kazuma."

"Then have Mr. Hyoizaburou sleep with him!"

"I'm sorry?"

Darkness was offering a sound argument, but Yuiyui seemed a little startled.

Hang on. I'm sure Darkness is right, but I get the feeling I'm missing something here...

"Well, we couldn't— I mean, knowing Kazuma from our daughter's letters, we couldn't let him sleep with Komekko—she isn't the right age yet. But I wouldn't be exactly comfortable letting him sleep with the master of the house, either..."

Hey, just what kind of person did this lady think I was? Tomorrow I was going to make them show me all the letters Megumin had sent them.

Darkness was getting more and more agitated. "Then...! Then have me sleep with him! At least if that animal tries to do something to me, I can resist with all my might, and somehow...! No! My resistance might be futile in the face of his inhuman lust, and he might do something awful to me. I-I'm sure his appetite has been building and building this entire trip. And he stayed up all night! They say men are especially ravenous after staying up all night…! He holds me down despite my desperate attempts to resist, blocking my mouth because *what if Komekko wakes up and everyone will hear and shut up already*—"

"*Sleep!*" Yuiyui intoned, and Darkness slumped down right where she was, ending the stream of idiotic inanities from her mouth. Good on Yuiyui.

…I looked at Hyoizaburou, who had somehow managed to remain fast asleep throughout this entire exchange. Maybe Yuiyui had…

That was when Yuiyui noticed me watching from the doorway. "Oh, Kazuma," she said, wrapping one arm around Komekko, who looked terribly sleepy. "Done with your bath? Miss Darkness fell asleep rather suddenly. Could you help me carry her to her room?"

The smile never left her face.

7

"Thank you for your help. Miss Darkness must have been exhausted from your trip. I'm sure she won't wake up till morning. And my husband and Komekko and I are all very sound sleepers. It's very hard to wake us up, even if there were to be any loud noises or voices or… Well, you must be tired, Kazuma. Rest well!" She kept shoving me insistently toward the room where Megumin was asleep.

"Uh, s-sure… Thanks, I guess I'll try to get some sleep… Hey, just so you know, Megumin and I have known each other long enough that there won't be any…mistakes or anything. Our pervy Crusader is just the worrying type. You don't have to listen to her, okay?"

"Oh, I understand, I know exactly what you're saying. And of course, on the off chance that anything *did* happen, I'm sure you would take responsibility…!"

You know, I don't think she understood very much at all.

She gave me one last, forceful push into Megumin's room. "Sweet dreams…!" I heard her say behind me.

I turned to the dark room, a little annoyed. There was Megumin. I had no idea when they had brought her in here. While she was asleep, I could see how beautiful Megumin really was. A few rays of moonlight filtered in through the window and played gently across her face. Looking at her rich, soft black hair, I felt a tugging on my heart that I had never…

…What was I doing, getting infatuated? I saw Megumin every day. It was probably trauma from that thing with the orcs that suddenly left me all googly-eyed over her. When we got back to Axel, I would have to go to the succubi for some psychological care.

I was pretty tired, and thinking about dropping off to sleep.

…And then I heard a voice from just outside our room:

"*Lock!*"

Megumin's mom must have magically locked the door. I knew it was mostly my fault for stupidly running my mouth about all the money I was coming into, but I had to wonder whether Mom quite had all her marbles. No matter how much their daughter had written, did they really trust a guy they knew only by letter? Maybe they had a lot of confidence in what she'd told them.

…*Whatever. Time for bed.*

It was only when I took another look around that I realized.

The futon Megumin was sleeping on was the only one in the room.

8

Bathed in the moonlight that drifted gently through the window, I froze. The sight of Megumin, snoozing soundly, filled my vision. It was just the two of us here now. Aqua had already drifted off to the sleep of the drunk, while Yuiyui had ensured the two most likely interlopers,

Hyoizaburou and Darkness, wouldn't be conscious for a while... And then she'd locked the door so no one could get in or out of our room.

Talk about the perfect setup.

There was only one bed in the room. And although it was spring now, it still got cold at this time of night. Even indoors, I would probably catch a cold if I slept without some kind of cover over me. And what if it turned into pneumonia or something? I had heard the healing magic around here didn't work on actual diseases. Death by illness was considered part of your natural life, and you couldn't even be brought back with Resurrection. In other words, it was way worse to die of disease than to get killed in battle.

Anyway, what was I worried about? It wasn't technically a problem for me to get under the covers with Megumin...

"............"

I stood thinking for a long time. If I so much as laid a finger on the peacefully sleeping Arch-wizard, I would never again be able to deny it when Darkness or Aqua called me a monster or inhuman or all those other hurtful things. I was a gentleman! Not some animal. But I did have her parents' permission. That meant I still had the upper hand, even if Megumin sued me or something. Or did I? I had no idea how this world's legal system worked. Damn! I should've studied the law more closely. Then I might...

No, that wasn't the issue.

It wasn't a question of lawsuits or something. I'd been looking at this all the wrong way. Argh! This whole situation had even me confused.

Okay, calm down, Kazuma! Calm down and think!

It was really a bit of a chilly night for thinking, though. It was hard to think when you were too cold. First I needed to get under the covers and collect myself.

I wriggled into the bed, careful not to wake Megumin. I felt the heat of her body beside me, heard her deep breathing. Now I could finally think…

....

No, I couldn't! What a cunning trap. I had ended up in bed next to Megumin without even realizing what I was doing. I was about to try to get up again when I realized. Suppose I scrambled out of the bed. I guess Megumin would open her eyes at exactly that moment. And then—well, you've seen enough anime and manga to know what would happen next.

Yup. No matter what I said, I would be sure to get it. And I could swear up and down that I hadn't touched her or that this was all her parents' doing, but it wouldn't matter.

Oh, man. This sucked. I was basically being framed as a perv.

Well, I wasn't going to make the mistake of all my forebears. If I could see how not doing anything was going to get me into all kinds of undeserved trouble…!

Then I can at least revisualize this and make sure it isn't a false accusation.

I could hear Megumin's deep, even breathing.

Oh man. My heart's really pounding.

It crossed my mind that I was about to do something totally unthinkable.

But hang on. I wasn't some sexless saint. I was just an average guy, and I wanted to get it on as much as the next virile young man. Put a healthy guy like me into bed with a beautiful, helpless, sleeping woman, and there was bound to be a, you know, "mistake."

It was Megumin's parents who had engineered the situation. It was all right—I could beat the rap. In this situation, I could walk free even if Sena herself took me to court…!

So I steeled my resolve and was just about to make my move when…

…Megumin opened her eyes, blinking sleepily. She saw me lying there, trying to make sense of the situation.

"Good morning," I said. "Did you sleep well?"

"Oh… Good morning, Kazuma… How long was I out…?"

It was late at night now—maybe not quite midnight but definitely a solid eight hours since Megumin had asked us to let her sleep for a while and then collapsed into bed. She gave a murmur of acknowledgment when I told her this…and then she suddenly seemed to register where we were.

"…And why are you sleeping in the same bed as me, Kazuma?" she asked, staring at the ceiling.

I, too, kept my eyes fixed above me as I replied, "…Don't make me say it. It's embarrassing."

"What?!" She suddenly sat up.

"Hey, don't steal the blankets; it's cold. Anyway, chill out."

"You expect me to be calm?! I wake up in my own room, in my own house, to find you in bed with me?! I couldn't be calm if—!"

As she spoke, Megumin jumped out of the bed and patted herself down. She was probably checking to see if I'd done anything to her.

As a relieved look came over her face, I said, "Geez, do you really think I'm so disgusting that I would do something to you while you were asleep? What is this vibe I keep getting off you people? We've lived together for more than a year, and has *anything* happened? Darkness, too—she was super against us sleeping in the same room like this." I straightened up the sheets Megumin had thrown aside when she jumped out of bed, letting only my head peek out from under the covers as I spoke. I was cold.

Megumin seemed a little lost for words at all this. "Er… W-well… You're right. I'm sorry… It's just that waking up to this was a little confusing... Y-you're right. You do jokingly sexually harass me, but you're not the kind of person who would actually do something untoward in a situation like this." The ghost of a relieved smile passed over her face.

Still not letting anything more than my head out from under the covers, I said, "Damn straight. And don't you forget it. The only reason I'm even in this room is because your mom trapped me here, okay? Shoved me right inside and locked the door with magic. Getting in bed with you was my only choice."

Megumin sighed at this. "That mother of mine...," she muttered, her shoulders slumping, as if everything I'd said made perfect sense to her. I rolled back the sheets and patted the bed next to me.

"So that's that. Get in bed—it's cold. Don't worry, I won't do anything."

This drew a momentary frown from Megumin. She looked at the ground and said quietly, "...You really won't do anything? Even though you've finally got me alone?"

Talk about suggestive. Wait—whoa. D-does she want me to do something? I mean, between this and the way she held my hand back at our campsite—I really am finally getting popular with the girls!

I immediately contradicted everything I had just said as forcefully as I could.

"Idiot, we're finally alone—how could I *not* do something? I've even got your parents' blessing!"

For some reason, this caused Megumin to run for the window.

"That's what I thought! I'm staying at Yunyun's house tonight!"
"Dammit! You set me up!"

Megumin jumped out the window of her room and disappeared into the dark.

Chapter 4 — May I Have a Just Cause for This Sleepless Night!

1

The next morning…

We saw Megumin's parents off to work and then had our breakfast. We were lounging around in the living room when Aqua turned to Megumin, who had come back from Yunyun's house, and said, "Megumin, Megumin! Since we're here, I want to do some sightseeing around the village."

"Sightseeing? You know this place is under assault by the Demon King, right?" I said in annoyance. Given the way the Crimson Magic Clan forces had walked all over the Demon King's army the day before, maybe it shouldn't have surprised me that Aqua would come up with the idea.

"Fine by me," Megumin said. "Since the village doesn't seem to be having any trouble, we could also just teleport back to Axel—but if you want to tour a bit, we could hang around here today and then go back tomorrow."

If that was how our resident Crimson Magic Clanner felt…

"Oh, hey, there's someone around here who can teleport back to Axel?" I asked. "Great, that'll make our trip home easier." Especially for me. This meant we wouldn't have to go back through the orcs' territory.

"You sound awfully happy, **Cad-zuma**," Aqua said. "All right, then. I'm going to have Megumin show me around. What does everyone else want to do?"

"Not a bad idea. I'm free; maybe I'll go with— Wait, what did you just call me?" I turned to Aqua, but she only gave me a puzzled look.

"Did I say something unusual?"

"N-no... Must've been my imagination...I guess...? Never mind. What about you, Darkness?"

She looked up from where she was making some repairs to her armor, but she didn't bite. "There's somewhere I'd like to go. A very skilled smith lives in this village. As a lover of fine armor, I want to pay him a visit. You have fun sightseeing, **Trash-zuma.**"

"Okay, gotch— ...What did you just say?"

"Just Aqua and **Ka-sleaze-ma**, then. This village has lots of interesting things to see, so you'll never get b—"

"Wait just one darn second!" I bellowed.

Aqua gave me another perplexed stare. "What's wrong, **Cad-zuma?** Upset your little trick on Megumin last night didn't work out?"

Apparently, the others had already found out what had happened the night before. I put my hands together in front of my face, bowing my head deeply. "I'm very sorry...!!"

But hey, I was a healthy young man—how was I supposed to resist in a situation like that? I mean, with a young woman in bed next to you, it would practically be rude *not* to do something, right? I explained all this to them as fervently as I could, but...

"I think you could do with another orc attack."

Megumin looked at me like garbage she was ready to throw out.

2

Some time later, after copious treats at the only café in town, Megumin was finally ready to be civil to me again. She brought me to one place in particular...

"The hell?"

Such was my first impression.

She had taken us to what seemed to be a shrine. "This is the guardian deity of this village," she said. I took a close look at it.

"This is a cat girl in a swimsuit."

The object of local veneration, housed deep in the shrine, was a figurine of a cute girl.

"Long ago," Megumin said, "one of our ancestors allegedly saved a traveler who was being attacked by a monster. In gratitude, the traveler gave him this and said, 'This is a god to me, more precious than my own life.' No one knows what god it is, but we venerate it like this just in case it helps at all. The traveler also supposedly told our ancestor how to build the shrine."

That traveler had to be Japanese. No question.

"Hey, Kazuma, it kind of ticks me off to see people worship a figurine the same way they're supposed to worship me."

"You're the one who sent him here with this thing. You owe the Crimson Magic Clan an apology."

Our reactions mystified Megumin. The next place she took us was…

"This is a holy blade said to bestow great power upon the one who draws it out."

"Now, that's more like it! I knew Crimson Magic Village must have some awesome stuff!"

She brought us to a stone with a sword stuck in it. And the chosen one who pulled it out would gain the legendary power of—yadda, yadda, yadda. You saw this sort of thing in games all the time.

"Hey," I said excitedly, "can I try?"

"Sure, if you want, but it'll be a while before it's possible," Megumin said. "Plus you have to pay a fee to the blacksmith if you want to try, and you only get one attempt, anyway. You should probably wait."

It'll be a while? Pay a fee to the blacksmith…?

"Oh, I get it. You mean it'll be a while until the seal weakens, allowing the chosen one to pull it out…"

"That sword is a holy blade our blacksmith made to bring in tourists. The magic that keeps it stuck in there will only break when the ten thousandth person tries to pull it out. So far we've only had about a hundred challengers. The smith made it roughly four years ago."

"Hasn't had very long to build up its legend, huh?" I said dispiritedly. Aqua went to take a look at the sword.

"Hey, I think I could break this seal with my magic. Can I take this home with us?"

"P-please don't. Our town needs all the tourist attractions it can get."

Megumin took us to a small pond shaded by trees.

"This is the Wishing Pond. There is a legend about it. It is said that if you make an offering of an ax or a coin, you can summon the goddess of gold and silver or something. Apparently, even today, people occasionally toss in axes or coins on account of this legend."

As legends went, that one sounded awfully familiar...

"We don't have the faintest idea who started the story, but if our kindly blacksmith didn't routinely dredge the pond, it would be a pile of metal by now."

"...Just out of curiosity," I said, "what does the kindly blacksmith do with all the coins and metal he salvages?"

"He recycles them into weapons and armor, of course."

I had a pretty good sense that I could finger the perp on that rumor.

"Now for our next tourist trap... Huh? Where is Aqua?"

Now that Megumin mentioned it, I didn't see her anywhere. Then, just as I thought I saw ripples on the surface of the Wishing Pond...

"...I take my eyes off you for one second, and look what you do!"

Our self-proclaimed goddess's eyes were just above the waterline. She must have dived in when I wasn't looking.

"Well, Megumin said there were coins down here, so I thought I'd have a look... Hey, when tourist season comes around, you could hire me as your temp pond goddess."

"Fine, I'm going to fling an ax at you. See if you can turn it into gold." I looked around for something to throw, but Aqua just splashed some water at me.

"Come on, you two—stop playing around. Let's move on!"

The next thing Megumin showed us was a totally normal-looking underground entrance. It seemed a lot like the entrance to a nuclear shelter...

"This is an underground facility that is home to a weapon that could very well destroy the world. When did this facility get here? No one knows... It's said to have been made at the same time as that mystery building over there..."

Megumin pointed to a huge structure of some sort. It was an enigma, all right... I wondered what it was. It seemed to be made of concrete.

"What's the mystery building?" I asked. "What's it used for?"

"It is indeed a mystery. What is it for? Who built it, and why? And when? All mysteries. Looking around inside didn't give us any clues, so we call it the mystery building."

What *was* it with this village?

"A weapon that might destroy the world, huh...? Could be serious trouble. But I guess the Crimson Magic Clan is made up of expert wizards. Any seal they put on it wouldn't be easy to break. There's probably no safer place for it," I muttered.

"Hey, Megumin, don't you have anything more, like, awesome sitting around here?" Aqua asked.

"You are just a bit too late. We used to have 'The Tomb of the Sealed Evil Spirit' and 'The Place with the Sealed Unknown Goddess,' but with this and that, the seals broke—you know how these things are—and..."

"The seals around here aren't worth squat, are they?! Is this world-destroying weapon really safe?!"

"Y-yes, it's fine. The seal on that building is a riddle written in ancient letters no one can read anymore, and you have to enter the answer in order to break it... D-don't look at me like that! I swear, it's okay!"

Megumin said there was somewhere she wanted to stop by and led us to a particular store. It appeared to be a clothing shop. The sign had some old clothes drawn on it, and through the glass door I could see a shop owner wearing a black robe and a baleful look. The owner glanced at us as we entered.

"Welcome to— Megumin. Hmm? Could those be out-of-towners you have with you?" He fixed us with an intense gaze. Aqua quailed under his stare and tried to hide behind me.

Wh-what was going on? Had we done something wrong? Maybe this guy had a bias against strangers or something. As my heart pounded, Megumin simply nodded.

This caused the proprietor to jump up, giving the cape he wore with his robe an impressively capable flourish despite the tight confines of the store.

"My name is Cheekera! Arch-wizard and wielder of advanced magic. First among the clothing-store proprietors of the Crimson Magic Clan!"

Apparently, there was a certain etiquette to introducing yourself here. After he had made this solemn pronouncement, the shopkeeper gave a satisfied smile.

"Again, welcome! My, but it's been a long time since we had travelers in here! How long has it been since I got to proclaim my name? Ah, that was invigorating. Thank you."

...They find that invigorating?

"My name is Kazuma Satou... So you're first among the clothing-store proprietors of the Crimson Magic Clan, huh? That's pretty neat."

The owner seemed to like this, because his grin grew even broader. "Indeed! Granted, this is the only one in the village."

"Are you kidding?" I spat out instinctively.

"There aren't that many stores around here to begin with, you see," he said. "I run the sole clothing store, and there's only one place to buy shoes. None of the other shops have any competition, either."

I thought I recalled Bukkororii saying he was the son of the foremost cobbler of the Crimson Magic Clan or something. Megumin saw me wrinkling my nose and looked away uncomfortably.

"Well, that aside, what brings you here today? Something you need?" Cheekera said.

"I'd like to change to a new robe," Megumin said. "Do you have any just like this? I got it from Yunyun a long time ago, but it's annoying to have only one."

At that, the proprietor took a careful look at his own outfit.

"A robe like that? I happen to have some, freshly dyed." He led us out to where the robes were drying on a pole. There were several that looked like the one Megumin was wearing.

"All right," she said. "Give me all of them."

"All of them? Ho-ho. I see your tastes have gotten more bourgeois, Megumin... Met some success as an adventurer, have you?"

"Well, do not be surprised if you start hearing my name around the village pretty soon. Anyway, this robe is rather my trademark, and I wouldn't want a bunch of people to run around wearing it... Hence, my soon-to-be-rich friend, Kazuma, kindly make with the cash."

"Y-you little... Hmm. I guess there's no telling when we'll be back here. Fine."

The shopkeeper, giddy with the thought of selling all his stock in one fell swoop, started gathering the robes off the drying pole. Now that I saw the simple rack more clearly, I couldn't keep myself from saying, "Hey..."

"...? Yes?" Megumin gave me a look as if to ask what was wrong with the apparatus.

"Are you—? I mean— What the heck is this thing you're using to dry those robes?"

"Ah, my dear customer, do you know what this is? This is a drying pole passed down in my family for generations. A precious thing that never rusts."

So the proprietor smilingly informed us...but when Aqua saw it, she said with great interest, "This is obviously a rifle."

And so it was. An imposing long-barreled rifle—just about the size of a drying rack, for which it was being used. I guess no one here would take it for a weapon.

Wait, though. The "deity" at the cat-ear shrine, this rifle, that concrete mystery building... Just what was going on in this village?

3

We left the store and wandered around the village some more, until we finally ended up resting amid the brush on a small hill.

"What a great view," Aqua said. "I should have packed lunches for us."

"If you want to drink in the scenery, there is an observatory on top of that mountain," Megumin said. "There is a magical item there capable of allowing one to see things that are extremely far away, so that we can peek into the Demon King's castle at any time. I am told the bedroom of His Majesty's daughter is a popular object of observation."

"You people really are good-for-nothing! You're even trying to make money off the Demon King's castle?"

"Hey, Megumin," Aqua called from where she'd sprawled in the grass. "This is nice and all, but you said you would take me somewhere with some ambience."

"There is ambience here! This is called 'the Devil's Hill.' Couples who swear their love to each other here are subject to the devil's curse and shall never break up for all eternity. It's a romantic tourist spot and very popular with lovers..."

"What in the hell is romantic about that?!" I demanded. "More like terrifying! Oppressive! ...Hey, what's that?"

From the hilltop, you could see the whole village clearly. And over by the entrance, a little to the side—just past the wooden fence next to Megumin's house, a dark shape was moving. I activated my Second Sight skill to get a better look, and...

"Whoa! Megumin, the Demon King's people are over there! Aren't they awfully close to your house?!"

Megumin's house was in a corner of the village, a little removed from the other residences. And just beyond the wooden fence there, a group that looked suspiciously like part of the Demon King's army was assembling. There was no warning announcement, which probably meant the Crimson Magic Clan hadn't noticed them yet.

"Where, where? They certainly are persistent, aren't they? To come right back after we beat them so soundly... I wonder what their objective is. From the way they're sneaking around, I doubt they want to attack people. Maybe they're trying to get to one of the buildings in the village."

One of the buildings...?

"Didn't you mention a tomb with a dark god sealed up in it or something? That sounds like the sort of thing the Demon King would be interested in. But you said the seal was already broken, right?"

"Unfortunately, yes. So I can't imagine what they would be after in our— Wait! Could they be trying to get to the deity in Cat-ears Shrine...?!"

"If that thing is really the Demon King's highest goal in life, then he and his army and this village can all just go to hell together."

But in that case, what *did* they want?

"What about that potentially world-destroying weapon?" I suggested.

"I doubt it. Unlike the other buildings, that one has a special seal, and anyway, nobody knows how the weapon is supposed to work."

Why did they even have something like that around here?

"Whatever. Nobody seems to know they're there. At this rate, they'll get into the village! We have to go warn everyone!"

"That's Kazuma for you," Aqua said. "Always big and brave, as long as there's someone else around to do the fighting."

I don't care. She can say whatever she wants!

4

We gathered everyone we met in the street and brought them back to Megumin's house. But there, we heard...

"What's this girl doing?! Where'd she even come from? What does she even want?!"

"Lady Sylvia! This woman won't go for help, and she doesn't have any powerful attacks—I don't know why she's even here. It may be a trap. Please stay back!"

The forces of the Demon King had broken through the fence, but now Darkness and her great sword confronted them.

"So long as I have sight in my eyes, you shall not pass!" she shouted. "If you want to get through here, you'll have to do it over my dead body—but I won't lose to the likes of you, so you are out of luck!"

"What a pain in the butt this girl is. No attacks but hard as a rock! She oughta just give up and run away! Lady Sylvia, let's forget about this freak and just do what we came here for!"

Apparently, Darkness had gotten home before us, had heard the enemy breaking in, and had been trying to buy us time. Stymied by Darkness, the Demon King's forces had breached the fence but couldn't get into the village. I wouldn't have expected Darkness to do something like that, and I had to admit with a touch of admiration that she had actually grown up a little.

"Way to hold them off, Darkness! We're here to help you!"

"K-Kazuma?! Aww, you're here already...?" She sounded down-right disappointed.

More fool me for being impressed.

"First the orcs turn out to all be female, and then the general of the Demon King around here is a woman, too!" she shouted. "All right, you! If you're really minions of the Demon King, then prove it! Over-power me! Make me call you Master or something!"

"Hey, quit while you're ahead," I shouted. "You almost looked really cool for a second there."

The Demon King types facing down Darkness paled when they caught sight of the crowd of Crimson Magic Clan members I'd brought along. Suddenly, their general—Sylvia, was it?—came out in front, as if to cover them.

"Impressive... You deliberately bungled your attacks, making us think you weren't a threat—and all the time you were just waiting for your friends to get here. Judging by the defense and endurance you've showed so far, you must be a pretty high-level Crusader... Was your total inability to hit any of my subordinates just another ploy to keep me from guessing your true strength? If we had realized how high your level was, we would've retreated a long time ago... Nice work."

"...Uh...yeah. I—I guess you sure...figured me out..."

Our little princess, trying to play off the enemy's mistake despite being a terrible liar, kept glancing to me for help. I had a whole squad of powerful Crimson Magic types behind me. Well, if they'd misread Darkness, maybe I could press home our advantage.

"Sylvia, right? That Crusader there is my comrade. She's an animal—she even withstood a massive explosion in our battle with Vanir. For you to grasp her true power in such a short time—well, I have to say, I'm impressed..."

"Megumin, why is Kazuma saying all that weird stuff?"

"Shh! It seems interesting. Let's see where this goes. Maybe he'll talk about us, too."

Beside me, Aqua and Megumin were whispering to each other.

Okay. Far be it from me to disappoint Megumin.

A shocked look came over Sylvia's face. "...Vanir? I'd heard he went to Axel Town and never came back. So *you*—?!" The Demon King's forces took a step back.

"Yup. Megumin here struck the final blow." That did more than startle Sylvia. It even set the Crimson Magic Clan people abuzz. Megumin got a little smirk on her face.

"That's not all," I went on. "The Dullahan Beldia. The Deadly Poison Slime Hans. Even that infamous bounty Mobile Fortress Destroyer...! We did 'em all in!"

"Y-you did what?! ...I'd heard Beldia had been taken down, but Hans? When—? But I guess his regular reports from Arcanletia did dry up not long ago, so it's probably true...!"

This village was just a few days distant from Arcanletia. It made sense that they would be in touch with each other. Now that she sensed some credibility in my words, Sylvia began gnawing fretfully on her lip.

"...You seem to be the leader of your party. Perhaps you could tell me your name."

M-my name, huh? I definitely did not need the Demon King's army learning my name. I could only assume there would be wanted posters out as soon as they could draw them up.

"...My name is Kyouya Mitsurugi! Remember it well."

"Mitsurugi! ...Yes, that makes sense. Mitsurugi, wielder of the magic blade. I've heard of you. You do have a rather odd sword with you. I suppose you must be him. Although I had always heard him described as an exceedingly handsome lady-killer, whereas you... To be fair, you're about *my* type... But with you here on top of these Crimson Magic types, I could be in real trouble. I don't expect you could find a way to let me escape for today?"

How polite of Sylvia to let herself be fooled by my sword into thinking it was Gram—Mitsurugi's weapon. As for Mitsurugi, I figured he could handle a wanted poster or two. Heck, apparently the Demon King's army already knew him by name.

"...He just can't come through when it counts, can he? And then he pretends to be someone else!"

"I guess he got a bit too full of himself with all these Crimson Magic people here. I'm a little worried..."

Stupid peanut gallery.

"I take your point," I said. "I'm sure we could finish off the lot of you right here, but then it might look like I only beat you because I had the Crimson Magic Clan behind me. And how would that burnish my legend? You may begone for today... That is, if my Crimson Magic friends agree?"

I gave a bold smile, and...

"Thank you kindly, Mitsurugi—catch you next time! Then we'll settle this! My name's Sylvia—general of the Demon King! Okay, everyone—retreat!"

The Crimson Magic Clan people went flying after her:

"Don't let her get away! *Lightning Strike!*"

"*Light of Saber!!*"

"Let's catch her and use her for our magical experiments!"

I watched Sylvia and her minions as they disappeared into the distance, and then I gave a deep and profoundly emotional sigh.

"The Demon King's general Sylvia, huh...?"

"Hey, Kazuma," Darkness snapped, "how long are you going to keep up that stupid act?"

5

"This is one awesome lady! Arrows, magic spells—they just bounced off her!"

That evening...

We were back at Megumin's house, where we planned to spend

another night. Dinner was over, and everyone was singing Darkness's praises for her work that day.

"A-aww, it was… Any Crusader could have…" Darkness was not used to this kind of adulation. She was sitting stiffly in a formal posture in the living room, accepting Komekko's comments with a show of intense embarrassment.

"We heard all about what you did, Miss Darkness—how you stopped Sylvia from getting into the village. What a brave and stalwart party! It gives us that much more confidence in entrusting our daughter to our dear Kazuma. Speaking of which, about the room assignments for tonight…"

Yuiyui sidled up to me as she spoke. But something was bothering me.

"Um, where's Mr. Hyoizaburou?"

"Oh, hubby said he had lots of work to do, so he was going to sleep in his workshop," she said easily. "Now I'll go get the bath ready." And then, in a flash, she was gone.

The way I remembered it, at dinner Hyoizaburou had said, "I'm worried about our daughter. I'll sleep with our guest Kazuma tonight."

…Was Mom at it again?

"In any event," Megumin said, "that little speech you gave was pretty cool, Kazuma. Next time we really will settle the score with Sylvia!"

"Yeah," Darkness said. "Actually, I visited the smith today—he's pretty talented—and I asked him to make me a new type of armor that he said is in vogue right now. It should be ready in a few days. Ooh. I'm looking forward to my armor and our battle with Sylvia…!" Both girls had their fists clenched.

To which I bluntly replied, "Don't be dumb. We're going home tomorrow, remember? We've seen all the sights and everything—there's absolutely nothing left for us in this village. Let's take off first thing in the morning. I can't wait to lounge around the house."

""Whaaaat?!""

Both Megumin and Darkness seemed surprised by this. Aqua, who was drinking wine and popping peas into her mouth, said, "After all that badass talk, you're just gonna run away? After she specifically said you would meet again?"

"Look, I admit I'm a little loathe to leave behind such a hot general, but we need to think of our personal safety here. A nice, cushy NEET lifestyle is waiting for us at home. Why would we go out of our way to stay here and tangle with a general of the Demon King?"

"Why— Why, you! You mean all that cool talk was only posturing?!"

"You had such a dramatic exit—and you're just going to go home?! That's ridiculous, even for you!"

"Are you kidding?" I said to them. "I took a stab at acting cool exactly because I knew we were going home tomorrow. I knew we wouldn't see her again. Why the hell else would I antagonize a general of the Demon King like that? I was in this nice, safe village with a whole squad of Crimson Magic people at my back. How else could I have done that?"

"This man is the worst! He is irredeemable!"

"You! Can you live with yourself as a human being?!"

Megumin and Darkness flung insults at me, but I just blocked my ears and ignored them.

"Everyone, the bath is ready," Yuiyui said, coming back in. "Oh… What's wrong?"

"Nothing's wrong," I said. "Hey, I call first bath."

"Hey! Don't you dare try to run!"

"This isn't over!"

The girls continued their abuse as I hightailed it to the tub.

When I got back to the living room after my bath, feeling refreshed, Aqua was making her way to her assigned room, looking almost as invigorated as I felt.

"Huh? Why do you look like you just got out of the bath?"

"I went to the one outside. They told me there was a bath right nearby—the one with the big sign that says *Mixed Bath*."

Wait a second, I hadn't heard about anything like that. And here we were going home tomorrow! What should I do? I was just wondering if I should delay our departure for another day, when...

"Megumin, where do you think you're going at this hour?! I won't allow a girl of your age to stay out all night! And you just came back this morning!"

"This house is the most dangerous place in the village for a girl my age! And anyway, you're just going to try to make me sleep with Kazuma again, aren't you?"

"Oh, Kazuma is a good match. Trust your mother. He'll be everything we hope for..."

"How blind must you be?! Wait. You do know what he's like, and you still— Oh, he'll be everything *you* hope for, won't he!"

I heard the dulcet tones of Megumin and her mother shouting at each other in the doorway.

"I don't know what's going on with them," Aqua said, "but I'm heading to bed. Seems like Darkness conked out after she got back from the bath, too." She gave a tired little yawn—maybe the wine had gotten to her—and retreated to her room.

I looked and saw Darkness, who had indeed fallen asleep in a somewhat unnatural position. This was definitely Yuiyui's work...

"This discussion is over! I'm going to Yunyun's house!"

"You'll never walk out that door! *Ankle Snare!*"

"Wh-what?! You would use magic on your own daughter?! And you call yourself my moth—"

"*Sleep!*"

A dull *thud* accompanied her voice. Yuiyui turned to me, all smiles.

"I'm very sorry, Kazuma, but my daughter seems to have fallen asleep in a most unusual place... Do you think you could help me carry her to her room?"

6

Oh man, what am I gonna do?

Seriously, this was getting out of hand. Next to me, Megumin was breathing evenly.

"Hey, Megumin. You're just pretending to sleep, right? I know you're awake."

There was no answer. Not that I expected any.

After everything that had happened the night before, I thought—maybe I should just go with it. I'd always been the kind of guy to just let circumstances sweep me along. I was already here; maybe I should just keep going.

I thought back to the time at our camp when Megumin had held my hand. As I listened to her breathe deeply in sleep, I gently took her hand under the covers. It felt cool and pleasant.

…I stopped and thought. If I went any further now, I would just be a common criminal. What I needed was a legitimate excuse for snuggling up to Megumin under the covers.

…A light bulb went on in my head.

The night before, when Megumin had woken up, I had explained that I was in the bed because it was cold. Well, I just needed to make it more than an excuse. I needed to bring the room to a temperature that would be unbearable outside our blanket. And I knew just how to do it.

Yes. Although I hadn't known it at the time, it was probably for this very moment that I had acquired this power. Still holding on to Megumin with my right hand, I popped my head and my left hand out from between the sheets and chanted some magic at the room's window.

"*Freeze!*"

I put my whole heart, and most of my MP, into the spell. It easily froze the surface of the window, creating a sheet of ice several inches thick. The temperature in the room immediately took a nosedive.

Yes! Perfect!

With the window frozen shut, Megumin couldn't escape through it like she had the night before. My plan was flawless. Sometimes I impressed even myself.

As I lay there, silently elated—

"…Hmm…?" Megumin stirred, maybe disturbed by the noise of my incantation.

"Morning. Did you sleep well?"

"…Good morning. Huh? Is this my room?" Her hand still in mine, Megumin looked around, still half-asleep.

Then she realized we were holding hands.

"—!! You've finally done it! You finally crossed the uncrossable line! Animal! Kazuma, you beast! I always thought you were a milquetoast who, though you might dabble in light sexual harassment, would never cross that final line even if you wanted to—but I see now!"

She practically flew out of the bed, ranting at me with tears forming in her eyes.

"Now, just a minute! I haven't done anything! Don't you think you're making a big deal over a little hand-holding? Look around—it's even colder than it was last night! I must have instinctively taken your hand so I wouldn't freeze to death!"

It was only then that Megumin seemed to notice how chilly it was in the room and started shivering. Then, after a cursory investigation of her own body, her face turned red.

"T-truly? That is, given what happened yesterday, I can't say I'm quick to believe you."

"Idiot. You know how long it's been since your mom dropped you with that Sleep spell? And I've completely behaved myself the entire time."

"H-have you really? I apologize, Kazuma, this was my misunderstanding. I should have realized. If you had the nerve to cross that line, you would have been all over Darkness long ago, as we have had so many party betting pools on… I'm sorry. It was rude of me to judge you like that." She was wreathed in a moonlight halo as she apologized.

"It— It's fine. But you know, you could do with thanking me one of these days. I mean, how often have I saved your skins even though it always just gets me in trouble?"

I was going to continue, *So this is the least you can do.* But when I looked at Megumin's face in the light of the moon, somehow the words wouldn't quite come out.

"…Thanking you? Yes, I suppose so."

Normally, when Megumin looked at me, it was with anger, or annoyance, or even pity. But right now, she wore an expression I rarely saw from her: the genuine smile of a fourteen-year-old girl.

H-huh?

Confronted with that smile, I suddenly felt an anxious twisting in my stomach.

"…Thank you for taking in a wizard who could only use Explosion and had nowhere to go in Axel Town back then. Thank you for always carrying me home when I use up all my magic and can't move. Thank you for letting me stay with the party, no matter how much trouble I cause."

Megumin was usually so prickly and confrontational. But suddenly she was pouring her heart out to me. Her skin, pale against her black hair, had flushed just a little red. Her crimson eyes—the source of her clan's name—shimmered, giving her a real air of the magical.

Seeing me flounder, she teased, "What's wrong? I just thanked you. You asked me to—and now you're getting all embarrassed?"

I was wondering the same thing. I actually found myself feeling extremely awkward. After the way she normally treated me, for her to suddenly offer such gratitude like this—well, I wasn't quite sure how to take it.

Despite my internal confusion, I said, "…Y-yeah, you're right.

Y-you know, I—I mean, we give each other a lot of grief, but you guys help me out an awful lot, too. To put it in Crimson Magic speak, I guess… **My name is Kazuma Satou. First among the weakest class in Axel and always getting in trouble. And one who will soon have a bunch of money, and then plans to live a fun and weird life with you guys…** S-so…I hope you'll hang in there with me."

Megumin giggled at the way I started to get embarrassed about halfway through, but she said, "And I hope you'll stick with us… Incidentally, it really is exceptionally cold tonight. Well, I guess the wind does come in through the cracks in an old house like this. You… You really won't do anything, will you? It's cold, and I'd like to get back in bed." Still a little red, Megumin nestled under the covers.

What with the feeling in the air, this gave me a fresh bout of anxiety. *Well, it is awfully cold. Guess there's nothing else to—*

…That was when I remembered the iced-over window.

How would I explain it if she noticed? I had suddenly and finally managed to raise my stock around here. If she saw that window, it would tumble right back down. What the hell was wrong with me? Why had I done something so impetuous and stupid? I'd gotten a little desperate.

As I lay there worrying about all this, Megumin cuddled right up to me. Much closer than when she'd just been lying there before.

"…M-Megumin, y-you're kind of in my personal space…" ·

Now I was anxious for a totally different reason than before, but Megumin said, "You're always more than happy to sexually harass me, but I snuggle up to you and you get a yellow belly? Anyway, you already said you wouldn't do anything, right? So what's the problem?"

Of course. No problem.

No problem at all.

But after that conversation, right when she seemed to trust me so much—if she saw the frozen window after all that, I had a feeling it was going to earn me more than a little name-calling.

While I was still thinking about this, I felt something chilly around my right hand. This time it was Megumin who had taken my hand in hers.

"...H-hey. Should a girl your age really be, you know—so aggressive? It's just like back at our camp. You suddenly do something like that, and my heart starts pounding... You know, I heard Darkness saying to your parents yesterday that putting you in a room with me was like putting a little lamb in a cage with a starving animal." I found myself sweating despite the freezing temperature. My voice had jumped an octave with nervousness.

Megumin exhaled. "Darkness said that? But she told me that you were a timid little rabbit who would just try to joke his way out of any situation when the opportunity really came up."

That bitch!

"Hey," I said, "what do you and Darkness usually talk about when you're together? I promise I won't get angry." Megumin appeared a little bit ill at ease, then pointedly looked away from me. "...Come on. I know it's got to be all no-good stuff."

"That's between us. A-anyway, let's get to sleep. We're going back to Axel tomorrow, right? We should get home early so we can take it easy."

Look at her trying to weasel out of this.

...Then Megumin, who had been so happy to burrow under the covers, said with a touch of embarrassment, "...I need to use the toilet," and climbed back out of bed.

...Hang on.

"Your mom magically locked us in again tonight, so—"

—we can't get to the bathroom, I was about to say, but Megumin gave a tired smile.

And then...

"That mother of mine. Oh well. I'll just go out the window agai—"

...she looked at the window and stiffened.

I covered my ears and buried myself in the blanket in a fetal position. Yes. This moment called for my Ambush skill.

Megumin, meanwhile, was looking blankly at the window.

"...Kazuma, what in the world happened here?"

"...General Winter went by earlier. Froze it right shut."

Megumin ripped off the covers I was trying to hide under. "What is the meaning of this, Kazuma?! *You* did this, didn't you? I know you did it, but I cannot imagine why! Why would you freeze my window?!"

Yow, was it cold without that blanket!

Still curled up, I tried not to look at Megumin.

"...If I tell you, will you promise not to get mad?"

"Explain yourself, or the ice on this window will seem warm compared to the frosty looks everyone will be giving you tomorrow morning!"

I confessed everything.

"...Kazuma, are you a complete moron? I can never tell if you are brilliant or an utter idiot. I take back all the gratitude I gave you earlier."

"There's nothing I can say. I have no idea why I did something so stupid, especially after yesterday."

Maybe all this travel was messing with my brain. Megumin gave the ice on the window a tap. I had put everything I had into that Freeze spell; it was too thick to break through with a little smack.

Instead, Megumin walked over to the door. "Unlock this at once!" she shouted, pounding on it. "Come on, open—! Mom! Mooooom!" But other than Megumin's yelling, the house was dead silent. There was no hint of anyone waking up.

Shivering, I pulled the covers back over myself. "Give it up. It's freezing. Let's go to sleep. Don't worry, I won't do anything—trust me.

And if you really can't wait to go to the bathroom, there's an empty bottle over there."

"What is it with you and offering me empty bottles?!" Megumin demanded, squirming. "And I might have trusted you up until a few minutes ago, but now I think you really are dangerous! Argh…!"

Man, what happened to those good vibes?

"Look, I'm sorry, my bad. I won't do anything! I was kind of confused when I froze that window shut, but I see how stupid it was now. I'm sorry," I said.

"At least get out of bed to say it," Megumin said in a defeated tone. Maybe the cold had finally gotten the better of her, because she crawled back under the covers.

"Whoo!"

Megumin interrupted my celebration. "Kazuma. This will come back to haunt you tomorrow morning." Her crimson eyes sparkled dangerously.

Well, a great man of the past said, "**Don't worry about tomorrow until tomorrow.**" That was sage advice. Megumin had taken my hand earlier, but now she lay as far away on the bed as she could and turned her back to me. We looked like a husband and wife going through a rough patch.

"…Hey. Aren't you cold? I sure am. Come closer."

"…Geez. It was so nice earlier. I wish we could go back to that." Megumin sighed.

As quietly as I could, I intoned, "*Freeze.*"

"Did you just say you were cold and then use ice magic?! Just how desperate are you to sleep next to me?" She sounded both frustrated and angry. "*Sigh*… There's only one pillow. You use it, Kazuma. But in exchange, I will borrow your arm." And then she slid up next to me.

"H-hey, after all that, you just glom on to me? I'm not— This isn't easy for me, either, you know."

Megumin, the covers pulled up almost over her head, buried her face in my chest. "I think I'll tell Darkness that you really are **a timid little rabbit who tries to joke his way out of any situation when the opportunity comes up**," she said, giggling.

...What?

Did this mean Megumin wasn't as upset as she let on...?

I knew it! It's finally my moment to be popular with the—!

And just as I was starting to get excited, my thin hopes were firmly shattered.

"The Demon King's forces are attacking! The Demon King's forces are attacking!! Elements of his army may have already infiltrated the village!"

...Ain't that just my luck.

7

The commotion, sadly, caused Megumin's mother to unlock the door to our room.

I left Megumin's house with only my sword at my hip—but when I left, who should I find but a badly injured Sylvia.

"*Pant... Pant...* Just a little— A little farther...! ...My, fancy meeting you here! Now I *am* impressed. I sent my minions everywhere, but you figured out where I was headed and came to stop me. Didn't you, Mitsu?"

"Cram it, lady." I edged toward Sylvia, holding my sword low, in nothing but my pajamas and my bare feet.

"'Cram it'? Magic sword or no, do you, a mere human, think to speak to me like—?"

"Damn right I do! Now pipe down, or I'm gonna beat you six ways from Sunday! I was having a *moment*, and you ruined it! Do you even know what time it is?! What the hell is wrong with you, bothering people at this hour?!" I cut her off and shouted at her as though I'd never been so angry with anyone in all my life.

"Oh! I-I'm sorry—!" For just a second, Sylvia looked genuinely abashed, but she quickly collected herself. "Wait a minute! That's some gall you have, scolding me. I'll teach you a lesson—you and your little friend there!"

At that, I looked behind me. At some point, Megumin had arrived, holding her staff. Sylvia's animal-like yellow eyes shone. At first glance, she just seemed like an attractive human woman, but I realized now that I wasn't sure what she was. I had seen her out and about during the day, so she probably wasn't a vampire. The tips of her ears were kind of pointy. Maybe she was a demon or something.

She didn't have any obvious weapons, but there was some kind of ropelike thing at her hip. I wondered what she used it for. Channeling my anger at having been interrupted in the bedroom, I stood in front of Megumin to protect her. Sylvia gave a little click of her tongue, a bewitching smile on her face.

"Oh my, could this be what I interrupted? I truly did wrong you." Even as she taunted us, Sylvia didn't take her eyes off Megumin and me. She kept glancing at my sword—she was probably still mistaken about who I was.

"Hey! What's all the racket? I'm trying to sleep. Did Megumin sleep-Explosion something?"

Aqua, apparently roused by the noise, abruptly appeared in the doorway.

"Aqua! The Demon King's general is attacking! Go get Hyoizaburou or Yuiyui!" That sent her scrambling back into the house.

I had my sword. I wanted a chance to get at least one good swipe in at Sylvia for ruining my moment.

"Don't think I'll go easy on you just because you're pretty! I'm all about gender equality—I'm not afraid to drop-kick a woman in a fight!"

"Aww, not going to hold back for little old me? I appreciate the compliment, though. I might just end up flirting with you instead of fighting!"

I wanted to use my trusty dirt-and-wind combo, but I had exhausted most of my MP on that boneheaded stunt earlier and wasn't in a position to do much spell-casting. I took the backpack I had grabbed when I came rushing out of my room and threw it to Sylvia as if passing a ball. She didn't try to dodge and caught it easily in one hand.

"Oh? What's this? A present for me?"

I followed up the pass by charging in with my sword, but despite virtually having one arm tied behind her, Sylvia managed to catch my sword with her free hand.

I know she's one of the Demon King's generals, but geez!

Now that she had my sword, she wasn't letting go. But a strange look came over her face.

"...This is your magic sword? And that technique—pathetic." She looked at me. "Are you really *the* Mitsurugi? Is this actually the enchanted blade Gram?"

Crap! My sword and my swordsmanship are gonna give me away... No, wait. Maybe I can keep bluffing...!

"That is Chunchunmaru."

"...Guh?"

Before I could say anything, the very bestower of the name broke in. "That sword is called Chunchunmaru. It is a storied and legendary blade. Please do not pretend it is anything like Gram, the *allegedly* magical sword whose real origin nobody knows."

"...Heh-heh. Ha-ha-ha-ha-ha! You aren't Mitsurugi at all, are you? Why don't you tell me your real name—and why you thought to hide it from me." Sylvia was laughing, but I didn't see what was funny.

"...My name's Kazuma Satou. I gave you a fake name because I figured if I told you the truth, you'd put out wanted posters for me or something."

"Ah-ha! Ha-ha-ha-ha-ha! Aren't you a sharp one! I think I like you."

She nearly bent double laughing. Something about my answer must have really tickled her.

That was when the door flew open again, and Aqua looked out.

"Hey," she called, "Megumin's mom was trying to wake up Darkness. I told her to come right away!"

Before I could answer, Sylvia tugged on my sword, which she was still holding. It was too sudden for me to let go; I stumbled forward, straight toward her. I hurriedly tried to drop my weapon, but it was too late. I went flying face-first into Sylvia's chest. She tossed the sword away and pulled me tighter into her bosom.

Thaaaank y—

Wait! This was no time for gratitude. This was a trap!

Even if I *did* have my face buried in a beautiful woman's giant, almost bare, generous yet somehow balanced bosom, that didn't mean— *Yes, thank you.*

I made some half-hearted attempts to resist, but—

"Just stay still! *Bind*!"

I was pretty sure I had seen that skill once before—hadn't a Thief adventurer used it? Could Sylvia be a Thief general of the Demon King?!

So it was that I found myself bound to Sylvia by the rope she had had at her waist, my head nearly submerged in her cleavage. It occurred to me that I would be perfectly happy to spend the rest of my life this way.

"I'll be keeping this boy as a hostage. I don't know why you didn't use your spells on me, little Crimson Magic girl, but if you try anything now, you'll take him with me!"

"Wha...?! K-Kazuma! Don't worry; you'll be— Ah, yes, you are indeed just fine. In fact, you look strangely happy." There was a cold gleam in her eyes. This was 100 percent not my fault, however, and I hoped she would help me. She could take her time, though.

"What's this?!" Aqua exclaimed. "You seem like some kind of demon! And I don't stand by and let demons take my— My— Hey, Kazuma, what *are* we to each other? I'm not sure what cliché to use in this situation! Anyway, I won't let you have him, even if he does look pretty pleased there!"

She fired some kind of magic in an attempt to stop Sylvia. I guess she wanted a catchphrase to say or something? This village must be really getting to her. I wanted to tell her to call me her irreplaceable friend or party member or whatever she wanted and just stop Sylvia—but with my face still in the valley between her breasts, it was hard to talk.

...On that subject, what had been going on with me recently? I mean, from the moment Yunyun had said she wanted my baby—first her, then the orcs, then Megumin and Sylvia. Granted, the orcs were kind of a negative, but there were definitely more pros than cons on this list. I guess it really was my moment to get popular. Or maybe my one redeeming feature, my good luck, had decided this was its time to shine.

In any event, I was stuck there between Sylvia's boobs when she said, "Your breath is getting awfully hot there, young man. You wouldn't want to overheat, would you? If you behave yourself, I'll give you a reward later."

Yep. Definitely my moment.

"A-actually, it's a little hard to b-breathe...!"

I was happy, there was no doubt, but I was also starting to suffocate. I was fumbling around, trying to find a good way to get some air, when...

"Sacred Exorcism!"

There was an explosion of magic from Aqua, who was trying to take advantage of Sylvia's momentary lapse in concentration. A huge, glowing pillar appeared around Sylvia and me and stretched toward the sky. Of course, it enveloped me along with her...!

"?! Aaaaaahhh!"

Sylvia made a startled sound and began screaming. But even though the demon-cleansing light had caught me up, too, I didn't feel a thing. Nothing happened to me—but in sharp contrast, Sylvia's dress was in tatters.

"Oh, now you've done it…! I had that dress specially made from the skins of lesser demons, and you ruined it…! Too bad for you I'm not some simple devil. That wasn't pleasant, but it was nowhere near fatal. A word of advice, though. The next time you attack me, this boy's life is forfeit!"

Pretty much half-naked now, Sylvia quickly broke my bonds, spun me around, and pulled my head back into her chest. Maybe she was responding to my protests that I couldn't breathe. How nice of her.

"My name is Sylvia! Chief of the Monster Strengthening and Development Bureau and one who has augmented and changed my own body! Yes—I am the Growth Chimera, Sylvia! And I'm taking this boy with me! Now, sweetheart, how about you and I become one again? *Bind!*"

…Now she's going 'My name is Sylvia!' too? I think she's been battling these people too long.

At her shout, the rope wrapped us up again. Frankly, with no weapon and my enemy directly behind me, there wasn't much I could do. So without any serious show of resistance, I put my hands up like I was giving a cheer and let the rope do its work.

"K-Kazuma! Give him back, you—! …Hey, Kazuma, you're not deliberately letting her tie you up, are you?"

"No," I said flatly, the back of my head pressed once more against Sylvia's chest. She was tall enough that even with my head at her chest level, my feet couldn't reach the ground. I just dangled there.

What was this sudden satisfaction and comfort I felt? It was like I had finally found the peace and stability I had been missing.

Megumin was just shooting me an ice-cold glare when I heard a familiar voice.

"Hrk...! How could I be caught so unprepared at a moment like this...!"

I looked toward the speaker. There was Darkness, appearing a bit Spartan without her armor, breathing hard. She wore only a thin black shirt and tight skirt and had her great sword in her hand. Yuiyui must have woken her up before she came running.

Darkness, the sleep still in her eyes, moved forward to cover Aqua and fixed Sylvia with a stare.

"Know this, general of the Demon King! The people of this house have already gone to call other members of the Crimson Magic Clan. It's only a matter of time before reinforcements arrive. So let go of that worthless young man you have pressed to your chest, closing his eyes in bliss, and be gone! And if you must take a hostage...please...take me! Take me instead of him! Please let me be your hostage instead of Kazuma!"

Sylvia gave an amused smirk at Darkness's outburst. "Goodness, what a nasty little boy. To have two such *close* friends! But, no deal. I've grown rather fond of him. Now, you—Kazuma, is that it? Have you ever considered throwing in your lot with the Demon King's army? I think you and I could get along very well." As she spoke, she gave me a friendly pat on the head.

"...Hey, what's going on here? When did Kazuma get so buddy-buddy with our archenemy? Look, she's patting his head and everything," Aqua said with an annoyed sigh.

"...Kazuma," Darkness said, "what are you doing there, anyway? ...Don't tell me you let her surprise you. I get it—her chest distracted you, didn't it? Sheesh, you're so predictable. Oh well, hang on, I'll be right there and rescue—"

"Ah, don't bother."

. . . .

""""""Huh?"""""

* * *

All four of them seemed taken aback by my rapid-fire reply to Darkness. Leaning my head into the luxurious sofa that was Sylvia's ample bosom, I said, "That's right. I said don't bother. Listen, all of you. Especially Darkness. You haven't exactly been very nice to me lately. But Sylvia here says she's fond of me! You know, it's been so bad lately that I was already wondering if it was about time for me to defect to the Demon King. How about you apologize? I work my butt off for this party—so apologize right now. Megumin already told me earlier how grateful she is for everything I do all the time. Come on, I haven't got all night!"

I was trying to channel Aqua when she wanted something. Darkness seemed flabbergasted. "L-look, Kazuma," she said. "That's not funny. A-and, well…maybe I have been a little rough on you lately. And maybe I should've been a little more generous with what I said about you to Megumin's family. I'm sorry. Oh yeah. You said a while ago that you wanted an award? Well, you really have done some good things. All right, when we get back to town, I'll—"

"Show me you mean it! You think you can win me over with some shiny trinket at this late hour? Take a look around. Miss Sylvia here is tempting me into the Demon King's army with a *very* generous offer, if you know what I mean. And what do you have going for you? Come on, tell me!"

Darkness, looking a bit shaken after I interrupted her, said timidly, "My… My defense?"

"Wrong! What you've got going for you is a seductive body that won't quit! Don't pretend you don't know what I'm talking about!"

"Hey, this guy is a lost cause. He's sounding really weird. I think we should just let the Demon King have him."

"I—I don't think we can. Whatever we may think of him, he does have a way of coming through when it counts."

Aqua and Megumin were holding a whispered conference. No

doubt they were plotting a way to rescue me. Darkness looked embarrassed; she seemed to be trying to cover herself with her hands.

"I—I don't…! I'm not trying to…*seduce*…!" She looked on the verge of tears.

"You damn well are!" I shouted. "Man, that body is wasted on you! Listen! Tonight, my Luck is as good as it's ever been! This may be the most popular I'll ever be with the ladies! So apologize! Apologize so that I don't just let my newfound esteem from the fairer sex lead me away with Sylvia! For example, you could… Yeah…!"

Psst.
The next two pages reflect the original
Japanese orientation, so read backward!

Sylvia, somewhat nonplussed by the stuff coming out of my mouth, put her hand on my head again.

"Very good... I can see you're as good a man as I took you for! Ooh, I really do want to take you back to the Demon King's army! But don't bully your little Crusader friend too much, okay? You should be a little more sensitive to a lady's feelings."

"For a demonic creature, you seem to know an awful lot about the heart of a human woman," Darkness said, glaring at Sylvia. "I can't begin to guess at a demon's age, but do you have a lot of experience as a woman?" Her sword was at the ready as she tried to draw Sylvia into battle.

"Goodness, but of course. I understand both sexes."

Ahhh, the wily ways of a beautiful demoness. Of course she would know it all...

Sylvia gave me another pat on the head.

"After all, I'm half man myself."

She said it as though it was no big deal.

"...Say what?" I asked uncomprehendingly, turning toward Sylvia.

Maybe something somewhere in the village was burning, because a faint light had come into the sky. It was just enough for me to notice something I hadn't before. On Sylvia's chin, and especially around her cheeks, there was just the slightest facial hair.

"Oh, didn't you hear me?" she said. In her pointy right ear, a blue earring sparkled... "I'm a chimera. This bust you seem so enamored of is something I whipped up for myself."

Again, as though it was no big deal. I struggled to pretend I hadn't heard her. I tried to keep myself from processing the words.

I mean... Didn't this mean...this was a *man's* chest I was so excited about...?

Huh... But...?

"...K-Kazuma?" Megumin asked uncertainly. "S-stay with us, all right? All right? Just hang in there. You're fine, just...stay calm..."

I thought back to something I had heard somewhere, long ago—of a man with a piercing in his right ear.

"You really are quite the man, though...," she said. "Why, just stroking your head like this, I can feel the excitement in my chest *and* my..."

The difference in our heights meant my butt was just even with Sylvia's nether regions. And...

"Miss, uh, Miss Sylvia... Maybe it's just my imagination, but it's almost like I can feel something...pressing against my butt..."

And with a certain embarrassment, Sylvia responded with the words made famous by so many manga and anime in Japan...

"Yes, *something* is."

My heart just about stopped.

1

"Wake up. Hey, wake up!"

Someone was shaking me as I came to. I guess I had just been having a nightmare. A nightmare where an androgynous demon with a sick sense of humor had...

"...Eeeeeyaaaagh! Stop, Sylvia! Stay away from me! I'll kill you! Don't think I won't!!"

"C-calm down, already! Don't get your panties in a bunch. I'm not going to *do* anything to you. I've already given those Crimson cretins the slip, so I'll set you free soon. You did let me go yesterday, yourself."

That eased my anxiety somewhat, though I still didn't let down my guard. It was then that I realized there was no one else around. The place we were in looked sort of familiar...

"This is the entrance to the storage bunker underneath Crimson Magic Village," Sylvia said. "The one they say has a weapon that might very well destroy the world." As she spoke, she took out some kind of magic item.

"...What's that?" I said warily.

"Hee-hee. Surely, a man like you at least has an inkling? Perhaps the name will give you a hint—it's called a 'barrier breaker.'"

I put two and two together in a hurry. "So that half-assed infiltration effort was an attempt to steal the weapon."

"Ah, I knew you would figure it out. This place is supposed to house a magical weapon of unimaginable power. And from what I hear, it has some special property that makes it especially dangerous to the people of this village."

Wh-what kind of weapon could that be?

"Yeah, but from what *I* hear, there's a special seal on this place that no one can break. And nobody knows how to use the weapon anyway."

"Oh really? Well, not to worry. The barrier breaker I have here is an especially strong one, even by demon standards. Even a seal placed by the gods themselves would— Huh? Th-that's strange..." Sylvia, crouched in front of the storehouse, sounded confused. "My barrier breaker isn't showing any reaction! What is this? This isn't a magical seal at all! N-now what do I do...?"

Sylvia was giving her item a dirty look. From beside her, I peeked at the so-called seal. It was a touch panel for entering a code, with alphabetic and numerical keys, as well as direction buttons like on a game pad. On the top part of the touch panel were words I recognized.

"'Ko-nami Command'...? Does it want you to enter the Konami code?"

"Y-you can read this ancient writing?!"

I didn't know what she meant by that. It was just regular Japanese. And the "Ko-nami Command" was just the Konami code.

"It's not ancient. This is how they write where I come from. It wants you to enter a famous cheat code, the Konami code, as a pass—"

I tried to cut myself off before I could say any more, but Sylvia grabbed my hand.

"You are an even better man than I thought. Are you saying you know the secret to cracking the seal that has thwarted even the Crimson Magic Clan and me?"

"I—I may be a pretty crappy adventurer, but still... Do you think I would really spill my guts to the Demon King's army that easily? You saw that Arch-priest with me. She can use resurrection magic, so nothing you can do can scare—"

"There are more ways to make a man talk than to scare or torture him. Hee-hee. My talents as a lover have been lauded as every bit as pleasing as those of a succubus. How long do you think you can endure my ministra—?"

Before Sylvia had finished talking, I'd punched in the code.

There was a mechanical rumble, and the heavy door began sliding open.

"...Are you sure you can live with yourself after that?" Sylvia said. "Well, never mind. I don't have time to waste anyway. It's so dark in here—I wonder what's waiting for us." She was trying to ready a light.

She had her defenseless back to me. I might not have had a weapon, but didn't she seem just a little *too* trusting? Although with nothing but my bare hands, Drain Touch was about the only attack I had available to me.

"Hmm? I wonder if I dropped it when I was running away. Well, shoot. I can't see very well when it's completely dark like this..."

Then it hit me. In this situation, there was no need to fight. I snuck up behind Sylvia.

"I'm sorry, but do you have a light or—"

I wasn't really listening to what she was saying.

Thump.

"Huh?"

I shoved her straight into the pitch-black storehouse.

2

"?! ...! ...!!"

I could hear Sylvia shouting indistinctly from the other side of the door, which was now safely closed again. She was pounding on it, too.

"Kazuma! Are you all right?! Where's Sylvia?!"

I turned around and saw Megumin and the others running up from behind me. I saw the familiar faces of Yunyun and Bukkororii, too—Megumin must have gone and gotten them.

"You guys missed all the fun. My brilliant idea means Sylvia is now trapped inside. It doesn't look like you can open it from the inside. Give her a month or so to cool off, and I bet she'll calm down."

Megumin seemed to be listening to the faint, enraged voice from within, then said, "Y-you locked her in?! Well, I suppose the weapon won't work, seeing as no one knows how to start it. But I'm amazed Sylvia was able to break the seal."

…I decided not to mention that I was the one who had gotten her in there.

"Y-you're going to leave her to starve? I know she's the Demon King's general, but don't you think that's a little bit too much?" Darkness seemed to feel real pity as she listened to the hammering from inside.

"Sylvia escaped us more than once—and you got her!" one of the Crimson Magic people said. "Well done, outsider!"

"These people have gotten the better of three different generals of the Demon King already. I guess Sylvia was no match for them!"

While the gathered Crimsonites heaped praise on me, Aqua said, "Hey, Kazuma, isn't there supposed to be a really dangerous weapon in there? Are you sure we should leave her with it?"

The Crimson Magic Clanners were quick to respond.

"Heck, even we couldn't figure out how to use it. What's Sylvia gonna do in there?"

"Yeah, if she manages to use that weapon, I'll do a lap of the village on my hands!"

"Now, then! Who's up for a drink?!"

"…Hey," I said. "What is it with these people? Are they saying that stuff on purpose? Does the Crimson Magic Clan go looking for trouble? Can they never be satisfied until they've tripped every flag they can think of?"

"W-well, I will not deny that my tribe likes to get itself into trouble. But don't worry. It's quieted down in there. Perhaps she ran out of oxygen."

I hadn't noticed until then that all the spitting and cursing from inside the bunker had stopped. I had to admit it gave me a bad feeling—but what could be wrong, huh? I mean, it was common knowledge that no one could work the weapon in there...

"Hrm?" Darkness said, shuffling her feet. "Kazuma, does the ground seem a little shaky to you?"

"Whoa! This is trouble! I've got a bad feeling! I think we'd better get out of h—!"

"Aww, what's the rush, Kazuma? We defeated another general of the Demon King. Hey, I know you kind of took care of this one on your own, but we're a party, so— I mean, you'll share the reward, won't you? Right? Heh-heh! I wonder what I'll buy with the reward for Sylvia!"

The sight of the increasingly giddy Aqua convinced me that something was definitely, for sure about to go terribly awry.

"Why does it have to be a flag with you every single time? Hey, Megumin, Darkness! Pull out! In fact, ask the Crimson Magic people to teleport us back to Axel right n—"

Even as I spoke, the earth seemed to swell up, and suddenly we found ourselves in a cloud of dust. And there in the hazy moonlight was...

"Ahhh-ha-ha-ha-ha! You really put one over on me, boy! Did you think walking out with that weapon was our only goal? My name is Sylvia! And as you can see—"

The lower half of her body looked like a massive metal snake.

"—I can merge anything, weapon or whatever, with my body! I am the Demon King's general, the one and only Growth Chimera, Sylvia!"

She gave a triumphant holler.

"Mage-killer! She's got Mage-killer!"

The Crimson Magic Clan people began screaming.

Mage-killer?

"Eeeyiyiyiyiyikes! This is bad, Kazuma—this is very bad! Let us get out of here, right this minute!" Megumin, pale-faced and lacking any of the bravado she'd shown just a few minutes earlier, was tugging desperately on my sleeve.

Wait a minute. I'd seen how powerful these Crimson Magic wizards were. Surely, they had some kind of trump card—?

"Gah! Not Mage-killer!"

"Forget the village! There's no hope!"

"*Teleport*!"

Or not.

"Megumin, tell me what is going on here! What's this Mage-killer? Is it dangerous? Is it the weapon that might destroy the world?!" I shook her violently, keeping half an eye on the fleeing wizards. Megumin had never been much for adversity...

"The weapon that might destroy the world? No, that's not it...! But Sylvia has merged with Mage-killer, which is almost as dangerous...!" This explanation came courtesy of Yunyun, looking every bit as pale as Megumin. "Mage-killer is the age-old foe of our Crimson Magic Clan—an anti-wizard weapon that's totally unaffected by magic!"

Well, crap.

3

We evacuated with the other Crimson Magic Clan members to the Devil's Hill, the one so popular with couples. From there, we looked out over Crimson Magic Village, now engulfed in flames.

"Our village... It's burning..."

I looked toward the source of the voice and saw a girl wearing a bandage over her eye like Megumin, watching sadly from the hill, as if fixing the image in her mind.

In the village, Sylvia, in her lamia-like form, had spewed fire from her mouth to turn the village crimson in another sense. Many members of the Crimson Magic Clan were capable of using Teleport, so there were no human casualties. But flames continued to devour the buildings of the village.

It hurt my heart to see it. Was it because I had broken that seal? But what choice did I have? And everyone had told me that nobody knew how to use the weapon or even start it...

"How in the world did Sylvia manage to break that seal, anyway?" I twitched at the voice. "Maybe she had a barrier breaker. But those aren't supposed to work on this seal..." As the voice continued, I surveyed the burning village, my heart pounding.

"Whatever the case," the village chief said with a grim look, "our only choice now is to abandon the village. I hate to let the Demon King win, but as long as we're alive, we can start again."

...Oh man. Things were looking really rough here. Was it all my fault? Was it because I had been so eager to get rid of the seal?

"H-hey, Megumin, can you really not do anything about Mage-killer or whatever you called it?" I said, agony in my voice.

"As I told you, Mage-killer is—as its name implies—an anti-wizard weapon. Magic has practically no effect on it. Once long ago, someone went on a rampage using it, and it is said that our ancestor was somehow able to destroy it using the weapon that is now kept in the underground storehouse. Since it was there, we decided to repair Mage-killer and seal it back up down there as a memento..."

"Why would you deliberately keep something so dangerous, and for such a dumb reason? ...Wait a second. Did I hear you say that you have a weapon that can counter Mage-killer?"

It was the obvious strategy. If you were going to use poison, you'd better have an antidote. They were keeping a way to destroy Mage-killer on hand, just in case. The ancestors of the Crimson Magic Clan must have decided to keep the weapon around, on the chance Mage-killer ever needed to be destroyed again. So if we used it...

But Megumin apparently read my thoughts. "...Kazuma. Nobody knows how to use this weapon that's supposed to be able to stop

Mage-killer. We do possess a text that should explain how to operate it, but even our village chief can't decipher the letters..." She kept her eyes fixed on the burning village.

This was the Crimson Magic Clan, known for their intelligence. I was sure they had given this a lot of thought. If magic didn't work on this thing, then honestly, I didn't have many cards to play. I could see Sylvia, transformed into something resembling a giant metal snake, tiny in the distance. If she wrapped those coils around anyone but Darkness, they would be crushed instantly.

...There just wasn't anything we could do.

At that moment...

"Hmm... Then I will play the decoy to draw off Sylvia. If I have the backing of some of the Crimson Magic wizards, she won't be able to do me in so easily."

This idiotic proclamation came, of course, from our resident muscle head.

"What are you talking about?" I asked. "Don't you understand that there's nothing we can do here? Are you just stupid? Even goblins know to stay out of a fight they can't win. Are you dumber than a goblin?"

"I-I'm going to have a few bones to pick with you when we get back to Axel! You'll pay for all these nasty things you've said to me! I'm telling you, I have a plan here."

...A plan?

"While I'm distracting her, you and Aqua sneak into the storehouse Sylvia demolished. You can both see in the dark, so it shouldn't be a problem. Then bring out that weapon."

"...Did you not hear the part about nobody knowing how to use it? Have you even been listening to anything we've said?" I asked in exasperation.

"Of course I've been listening," Darkness said, "and before you ask, I understood it all, too. But if we can figure out how to work the weapon, maybe we can do something. If there's any chance at all, then it's better than standing here, twiddling our thumbs. Don't worry—I don't know what exactly this weapon is, but as the daughter of nobility, I know much about magical items. I once broke my father's magical camera and put it back together, you know."

I had to admit, it wasn't what I'd expected from Brawn for Brains. I stood there reeling with surprise.

"...That is a good idea," Megumin said. "Let us try it." This surprised me, too. I would have expected her to be more opposed than anyone.

"I've always liked a good high-stakes twist!"

"Yeah, my favorite thing! For outsiders, you sure seem to understand a lot about us!"

Not just Megumin, but all the Crimson Magic people seemed to be getting on board. Darkness's idea seemed to play right to them. Normally, I would have had no part of something so dangerous, but I couldn't get the girl with the bandaged eye out of my mind.

Dammit. Fine. I would just go in there, get the weapon or whatever, and get out. If that was what it took to clear my conscience...!

"Hey, there's a general of the Demon King running amok in that village! Count me out! I'm a support type; I do my work from nice, safe places like this hilltop!"

"Oh, shut up and come with me! I'm not finding that thing on my own."

And so I dragged Aqua, kicking and screaming, toward the underground storehouse next to the mysterious building...!

4

In order to draw off Sylvia, the Crimson Magic wizards attacked her with magic from afar. When she got too close, they would widen the distance again before returning to the assault. But magic really didn't affect her, and they were doing no damage.

"Resistance is futile. Haven't you had enough? I thought you all were supposed to be smarter than this," she taunted them, coiling her metal body. Now that she finally held the upper hand, Sylvia seemed intent on tormenting them to let off her anger. But for all her jeering, she wasn't able to get close enough to the wizards to land an attack, and she seemed to be getting tired of it.

She moved awfully slowly—maybe she wasn't used to her new snake body yet. She turned toward a group of wizards and took a breath. Her eyes were filled with death and hatred, and she breathed out a stream of searing flame. But instants before the fire enveloped them, one of the members of the group chanted a spell.

"*Teleport*!"

And they simply disappeared.

The groups combined teleporters and attackers, with the teleporters preparing their chants ahead of time so the spell could be invoked at any moment.

Sylvia, infuriated by her prey's escape, turned her eyes on a lone girl. She was the closest one to Sylvia, but Sylvia hadn't been able to focus on her during the magical drubbing. Now she gave chase. Apparently, she'd decided to take the wizards out one by one.

A man watching this from afar gave a scream. It was Bukkororii, leader of the anti–Demon King strike patrol.

"S-Sylvia, stop! I beg you! Don't lay a hand on her!"

Sylvia's quarry stood with a wooden sword in hand, drawing a bead on her enemy. I thought I recognized her. Hadn't she been using really powerful magic to fight the village's attackers alongside Bukkororii? She must have been his girlfriend or something.

Bukkororii had fallen to his knees imploringly, looking at Sylvia and the girl who faced her. Hearing his pleas, Sylvia broke into a grin of unbridled joy.

"This from the ones who so gleefully murdered my own minions. Consider this payback! Oh, but don't worry. I won't stop with this girl. I'll kill you and your family! I will burn this village to the ground! …Now prepare yourself!"

Sylvia ignored Bukkororii's howl, closing in on the girl. After being at the mercy of the Crimson Magic Clan for so long, she was finally going to be able to get her revenge.

The girl holding the wooden sword flashed a brave smile and called out to Bukkororii, whose expression was growing darker by the moment. "Run... At least one of us should escape. I shall expend the last of my strength against Sylvia so that you can flee!"

Aww, for crying out loud! I break that seal to save myself, and now people are getting hurt...!

Sylvia stood ready to attack. The girl stared back at her with intense resolve.

"I've still got an ace up my sleeve, Sylvia! Take a good look! And..." She glanced over at Bukkororii, and the most fleeting of smiles crossed her face. "Please, Bukkororii... Forget about me. Live your life; be happy..."

"Soketto, how could I ever?! Please, Sylvia, stop this! Soketto, I I—!!"

Geez, that's enough! Enough already...!

"I like a girl with spunk. Show me this ace of yours! No magic can hurt—"

"*Teleport!*"

As Sylvia shouted, the girl called out the word and disappeared. At that, Bukkororii, who had looked like a broken man just a second before, stood up, brushed himself off, and gazed calmly at Sylvia.

Sylvia, having lost her target just as the battle was heating up, muttered forlornly:

"I hate you Crimson Magic Clan people."

...I feel ya.

5

A Crimson Magic man stood in front of Sylvia, blocking her way. With a somber expression, he said, "**Sylvia. What a terrible form you've**

assumed. Now I shall have to use the ace up my sl— Eeeyow! H-hey, that's hot! It's only polite to let a person finish his dramatic monologue before you attack him!"

Sylvia had interrupted him in the middle of his proclamation with a blast of her fire breath, and he scrambled to get out of the way.

"I don't have time for your little games anymore! If you don't want to fight, then you'd better disappear for good!"

Sylvia was beginning to lose her cool at the Crimson Magic Clan's hit-and-run tactics. But she was far enough from the underground storehouse. Now was our chance. I would have liked nothing better than to run away, but it was my fault the seal had been broken.

"Okay, here we go. Darkness, if those wizards get themselves in too much trouble, you take care of them. They're powerful, but they're still wizards. When they run out of MP, they won't be able to use Teleport to escape anymore."

"I understand. You can count on me!" She gave a firm nod.

Beside her, Megumin asked, "Wh-what should I do? I cannot use Teleport, so I don't know if there is much I can do to buy time..." She looked up at me uneasily.

"We're keeping you in reserve in case we really need you. You said Mage-killer isn't impervious to magic, just very hard to damage with it, right? We know advanced magic doesn't work, but has anyone tried using Explosion on it yet? It might just be enough to do damage."

That was the excuse I gave her anyway. I didn't want to make her use her magic this time. I remembered what Yunyun had said, how bad it would be for Megumin if the villagers discovered she could use only Explosion.

My bluff must have worked, because Megumin gripped her staff tighter as her breathing intensified. In the distance, the Crimson Magic Clan wizards were still distracting Sylvia...

"Ah-ha-ha-ha-ha-ha! What's wrong? Let's see just how fast you can teleport!"

"Wait, I'm not done chanting—! Everyone, watch out! She's getting quicker!"

...Uh-oh, Sylvia was more used to her body now. The wizards weren't really distracting her anymore; she was simply chasing them.

"Okay, Kazuma, just leave protecting the storehouse to me. You can look around inside in perfect safety."

"Stop trying to ditch me and come on!"

I grabbed Aqua, who was determined to weasel out of her part in the plan until the bitter end, and used Ambush to allow the two of us to sneak past the magical battle with Sylvia.

At length we arrived at the bunker and entered through the hole Sylvia had made getting out. A glance back at the general herself showed that she was still focused on chasing down the Crimson Magic Clan. Maybe it was the nearing dawn that accounted for the light I could see on the far side of the mountain—but inside the bunker, it was pitch-black.

Aqua and I, both capable of seeing in the dark, slipped into the underground storehouse. Now we just had to find the—

"...Geez. We're supposed to find that thing in *here*?"

The storehouse was an absolute mess of magical items. We didn't know whether the weapon was even here, let alone which one of these things it was...

"Hey, Kazuma, hey! Look at this!" As I stood there fretting, Aqua happily brought me something she had picked up. I took a look...

"If it isn't a Game Girl! What's an ancient piece of gaming equipment like that doing in a place like this?" It was a portable gaming device that had been popular in Japan before I was born.

Aqua set the thing on the floor and started rummaging through a pile of magical items. "If there's a game system, there must be games around here. Hey, Kazuma, if we find a copy of *Ristet*, can I have it, please? I'll let you play."

"We're not looking for video games; we're looking for a weapon! Do you see anything weapon-y around here? ...Wait, what even is this place? Why are there so many things from Earth here?"

The vast majority of the magical items were actually various kinds of video-game machines. As a gamer, I felt my heart skip a beat, but this wasn't the time. All the consoles seemed a little off, too, as though an amateur had been struggling to make them…

Aqua beckoned to me from a corner of the room, where she seemed to have discovered something.

"Kazuma, look what I found." She showed me a diary. I came up beside her, peeking at the pages. They were full of what the Crimson Magic Clan people would have called ancient letters.

…That's right. The diary was written in Japanese.

Aqua began to read…

Month Such-and-Such, day So-and-So. Crap! They found out about this building. Luckily, they don't seem to understand what the things are that I've made. If they realized I had spent the country's research budget creating video games and toys, who knows what they'd do to me?

I started connecting the dots. Some Japanese guy who got sent here before me must have set up this facility. That was why you had to enter the Konami code to get in. Maybe this diary would offer some kind of clue for us.

Month Such-and-Such, day So-and-So. The bigwigs who barged into my paradise wanted to know what my game was good for. I could hardly tell them it's just for amusement. So I put on the straightest face I could muster and lied through my teeth. I told them it was a weapon that could very well destroy the world. "Th-this…?" asked one of the researchers. She flipped the switch on the Game Girl, and I could see her jump when it went da-ding! *She's a tough lady—and she's afraid of a little game machine?*

…?

Why was my stomach twisting?

*　　*　　*

Month Such-and-Such, day So-and-So. They told me they were going to dramatically expand my budget. In return, I was to create a weapon that could fight the Demon King. Seriously? I've already made more than enough use of the cheat I got when I was sent to this world. I've done my part for this country. They can ask for whatever they want—but it won't do any good. I put on my most serious face and said, "War will not solve anything," etc., etc. But my colleague just gave me a smack. She huffed that we were "at war with the Demon King" and I "had work to do." And that's true enough. But what the heck kind of weapon could fight that monster?

I had a bad feeling, all right. I remembered the last time we found a half-assed diary like this… But bad feeling or no, Aqua read on.

Month Such-and-Such, day So-and-So. I think I'll make a giant humanoid robot. One that can transform! I submitted the plans, but they angrily told me to be serious. Even though I was being serious! I just stuck a finger up my nose and shot back, "Well then, we'll just make it huge and resistant to magic." And they went along with it! Is that really all it takes? They told me to draw up some blueprints—but what am I going to model it on? …Huh? Is that a stray dog? And not a moment too soon. He's perfect. It'll be a dog-shaped weapon, and I think I'll call it "Mage-killer."

…Dog-shaped weapon?

Month Such-and-Such, day So-and-So. The higher-ups were very happy with my blueprints. They said, "Ah, yes, a snake. Much easier than having to build legs. Excellent idea." Excuse me, but that's supposed to be a dog. I know I'm not the best artist, but are they blind? It's a dog with a long metal body… Actually, I guess it does kind of look like a snake.

*   *   *

....

Month Such-and-Such, day So-and-So. Testing has begun. I got it to move, but the battery just doesn't last. I pitted it against some members of the Magic Clan, but it quickly stopped moving. They all seemed to be pretty scared of it, though, for no apparent reason. That's great. I'll tell them this weapon is too powerful to leave in human hands and shut it up in this building. It has no batteries, so it won't work, but maybe someday I can make it part of a chimera and turn it into a living weapon. Then it wouldn't need batteries, plus that would be wicked cool.

Okay, I think I'm starting to get the picture. The guy who wrote this diary was probably the same guy who built...you know.

Month Such-and-Such, day So-and-So. I've come up with a new weapon to fight the Demon King. Well, it's really just a human modification. I asked around this country for volunteers to undergo augmentation surgery, and I got so many applicants, I had to pick by lottery. They're practically obsessed with modifications here. Are they sure about this? I told them their memories would be gone after the surgery. I explained to my participants that it was just a simple procedure to allow them to use magic to the greatest possible extent. They, in turn, asked me for all kinds of ridiculous things, like could I also make their eyes red, or could I put serial numbers on them or something. Does everyone around here think like this?

It had better be the same guy, because I would hate to think there was more than one person out there who would write crap like this.

Month Such-and-Such, day So-and-So. The augmentation is finally done. My subjects came to me saying, "Master, give us new names." Who the hell is this "master"? Why are they so into this? I didn't want to be bothered, so I gave them random names. They seemed awfully happy about it, though. I kind of wonder about their sanity. But they're strong—really strong. The bigwigs seem happy again. I'm moving up in the world—I'll be head of research starting tomorrow. Frankly, I would rather have a nice, fat bonus than a fancy title. Since I'd gone to the trouble, I figured I would give a name to these enhanced people. I called them the "Crimson Magic Clan," after the color of their eyes. My colleague told me that was way too obvious. Damn her.

"Whaaat?!" I exclaimed without meaning to. Aqua stopped reading and looked at me. "S-sorry," I said. "Go on." The Crimson Magic Clan were modified humans? This had gotten really heavy all of a sudden...

Month Such-and-Such, day So-and-So. The Crimson Magic Clan members are begging me for a weapon to counter Mage-killer, which they consider the greatest threat to their existence. I mean, it doesn't even work. I didn't build it to threaten them, and it doesn't have any batteries. But no matter how many times I explain this to them, no one will listen to me. What is this, the enhanced human equivalent of the "terrible twos"? Fine. I built them a weapon. I wasn't going to think too hard about it at first, but I got a little too into it, and it's actually something now. Maybe this weapon really could destroy the world. It's kind of a laser cannon. It doesn't use electromagnetic acceleration or anything, but I can't come up with a good name, so for the moment I'm dubbing it the Railgun (tentative name).

...Okay. Not so heavy.

Month Such-and-Such, day So-and-So. My Railgun (tentative) is awesome. Super awesome. Honestly, it might be too awesome to handle. I meant for it to be a simple weapon shot with compressed magic, but when I let the Crimson guys fire off a round, I was surprised by just how destructive it was. It was downright frightening. It probably won't have power like that for long, though. I just kind of threw it together from whatever parts I could find. It looks likely to just fall apart after a few shots. It could be really dangerous in the wrong hands, though, so I think I'll shut it up here, too... Actually, the length is almost exactly right for a drying pole. Man, am I in trouble now. Everyone is riding high because the "Crimson Magic Clan" thing worked out so well, and now the higher-ups want to use their exploding national budget to build a supersize mobile weapon. Do they think it'll be that easy? What a bunch of morons. Not that it has anything to do with me.

...Welp, no doubt now. The author of this diary...

"That looks like the end... Hey, I think I recognize his handwriting from somewhere."

...was definitely the scientist who built Mobile Fortress Destroyer and then went full skeleton inside it. Judging by what he wrote here, he must have gone on to build it after this.

"Of course you do. You read the diary in Mobile Fortress Destroyer, right? It's got to be by the same guy."

At that, Aqua gave an excited clap of her hands. Did she have a special talent for identifying handwriting or something?

...Hang on a second.

"Hey, so was the diary we found on Destroyer written in Japanese, too?"

"Uh-huh."

"What do you mean, *Uh-huh*? You didn't think you should mention an important fact like that?!"

"Y-you never asked!"

I pressed my fingers to my aching head. "Dammit! So you're telling me all this—Destroyer, Mage-killer, everything—was because of some OP Japanese guy you randomly sent here, whose name you can't even remember?! You would send a ham sandwich here, wouldn't you?!" I stopped dead. "Just a minute."

Aqua gave me an inquiring cock of her head.

"I never really thought about it before, but just how old are you, anyway? You have to have been a goddess since at least before Mobile Fortress Destroyer was created."

Aqua dropped the diary on the ground with a *thump*. "...Kazuma, what kind of answer do you expect, asking a goddess her age? You're seriously headed for divine punishment, you know that? ...Let me explain something to you. That room where we first met? The flow of time is slowed way down there. Meaning it's not even possible to express my age in years as you know them. Okay? So don't ask again. You try another question like that and I really will give you a taste of divine retribution, Mr. Kazuma Satou."

She sounded unusually serious. I muttered, so quietly that she might or might not hear me:

"I get it. You're old, huh..."

"Whaaaaat?! You take that back! Who are you calling old?! Time is slower where I live than where you live, so I've been around longer than you, that's all! Take it back! Waaaaah!"

Everything I laid eyes on here was something that, as a gamer, I was desperate to take home with me. But this wasn't the time. I was pawing through the mountains of gaming equipment, looking for the Railgun (tentative).

"Dammit, where is that stupid Railgun? He said it's the size of a drying pole; there's no way we could miss it!"

"Hey, Kazuma, time moves differently in Japan than in the divine realm or even here. For example, a month in Japan is just about an hour in the divine realm. But it could be several months in this world. You see? So when it comes to my age... Hey, are you listening?"

Aqua had been going on with what sounded like excuses for a while now.

"I don't care about that! Just help me look, already! Do you see a rail gun anywhere? About the length of a drying pole..."

…The length of a drying pole?

Rail gun?

Hang on. I was pretty sure we saw something that fit that description somewhere in the village not too long ago. Yes! At the clothing store, the one Cheekera ran…!

"Aqua, I've got it! I know where to find the weapon!"

But as I turned toward Aqua…

DA-DIIING!

"Hey, look, this works. It seems to use magic instead of batteries, though. I wonder how many games it has? I'd love to take them all home."

I silently took the game machine from her, raised it way over my head, and…

"Graaaaaaahhhhhh!"

"Nooooo! My Game Girl!"

6

I dashed through the village, burning embers swirling through the air.

…And I could hear Aqua's shrill voice behind me.

"Give it back! Give me back my Game Girl! We'll probably never be able to get another one in this world! You owe me big! You have to pay me back with the money you get when we go home! Three hundred million is cheap as the price when you consider that was an irreplaceable, one-of-a-kind object!"

"Will you shut up about the games already?! We've got bigger problems! And it wasn't yours anyway—you just found it on the ground! How can you be so much older than me and still act like a spoiled child?!"

"Ooh, you're really pushing it, mister! I told you, celestial beings don't age! You'll regret ticking off the goddess of water! I'll curse you so your toilet doesn't flush, and your shower suddenly turns cold, and…!"

I ignored Aqua as she listed off the infantile "divine punishments" she planned to inflict. In the meantime, we finally arrived at the clothing store.

In the garden, the dull silver rifle-slash-drying-pole was waiting for us. From Destroyer to Mage-killer, the guy who built this stuff clearly had a homicidal streak. What was this doing here, anyway? They should be stashing it somewhere safe. What a bunch of idiots there were in this village. I could lecture them all day about using something this dangerous to dry their clothes.

The gun was a bit over three meters long. I tried to lift the shimmering silver weapon, but it was too heavy for one person to carry alone. I had Aqua help me.

There was some ridiculous-looking thing stuck to the back of the rifle, maybe a device to absorb magic. Railgun was a laughably obvious name for this thing, but it did have the look of a futuristic weapon.

"Okay, now we just have to get this back to the Crimson Magic Clan people, and… Huh?"

I suddenly noticed a vague sense of apprehension in my chest. The sounds of destruction that had been so prevalent a moment before had gone quiet. I looked around in confusion, and it was easy to spot Sylvia's massive body in the village. Far in the distance, she had come to a stop.

7

We brought the rifle closer to Sylvia, taking care not to be noticed. She had gone stock-still and was staring intently at a single point. And what she was staring at was…

"Isn't that Yunyun?! What is that girl thinking…?"

There was Yunyun, standing on a huge rock and glaring down at Sylvia. I had a notion why she was facing down Sylvia all alone. The other Crimson Magic Clan people were out of MP. But that didn't seem to be the only reason they were all gathered around to observe.

"Yunyun…"

"Yunyun is going to…!"

"Yunyun, the daughter of the chief, will…!"

They were watching her the way you would watch your personal hero. In the midst of it all, one of them muttered, "Yunyun's a weirdo who's embarrassed to even proclaim her own name. What's going on here…?"

Aqua and I watched, too, swallowing heavily.

Sylvia closed the distance, flashing Yunyun a taunting smile. And here I'd thought she was through letting the Crimson Magic Clan provoke her. What was this? My questions were answered by the conversation that followed, as well as the object the girl showed to the chimera.

"…It's true. The Skills field on your Adventurer's Card doesn't show any spells for teleporting through space… But are you sure you should have told me that you don't have any way to run like a scared little animal?"

I didn't know what they had said to each other before we arrived, but I could take a good guess. Yunyun had gotten Sylvia's attention by telling her that she was unable to teleport. Sylvia, after all, was clearly sick of having the Crimson Magic wizards disappear on her at the last second. And now Yunyun was deliberately admitting that she couldn't. That rock looked like a difficult spot to escape from, too. She might be able to jump down, but even if she hit the ground running, she would never get to her friends before Sylvia caught her. I knew all about charging in headlong, but this was ridiculous…

I was about to call out to Yunyun when I felt a tug at my elbow. I looked and found that Megumin had arrived, leading Komekko by the hand, along with a dejected-looking Darkness.

"Kazuma," she said, "did you find the weapon? When we realized

Komekko was not at the evacuation point, Yunyun decided to distract Sylvia like that to buy us time to go back to the house and get her..."

I looked at Komekko. She seemed a little dazed; she had obviously just woken up. Apparently, she'd slept through the entire commotion until just a moment ago.

That girl was going to be trouble one day.

"I'm glad you were able to get her. You'll be happy to know that we found the weapon. But what's with you, Darkness? Did something happen?"

"At first I was able to bait Sylvia just like we planned, but... But before long, she said she didn't have any interest in fighting a woman who was all defense and no attack..."

Aqua patted Darkness's hanging head.

Apparently, once Sylvia had realized Darkness couldn't actually fight, she'd decided to go somewhere else.

Well, we had more important things to worry about.

"I get it; everything sucks right now. But listen, we have to help Yunyun before—"

"No!" Megumin said. "You must not interfere! She has something up her sleeve. It's all right. Judging by the flattened grass around that rock, help is already there. Let us simply watch!" Her eyes shone with anticipation.

Help was already there? But it didn't look to me like anyone was even trying to get close to Yunyun.

For some reason—maybe because the rock she was on came to such a narrow point—Yunyun was standing on one leg like a crane, perfectly balanced.

"My name is Yunyun! Arch-wizard, wielder of advanced magic..."

Then, just for a second, she glanced at Megumin, standing next to me.

"...first among the spell-casters of the Crimson Magic Clan, and she who will one day be chief of this village!"

"What did she call herself?!" Megumin exclaimed in shock. It looked like there was a bit of rivalry for the title of first among the Crimson Magic Clan spell-casters.

All crimson eyes were on Yunyun. Her usual timidity was gone. She whipped back her cape in a dramatic flourish.

"Sylvia, general of the Demon King! As the daughter of the chief of the Crimson Magic Clan—I shall show you a secret spell known only to members of the chieftain's line!"

With one hand, she raised her wand high, then murmured something briefly to the heavens. She must have incanted some kind of lightning magic ahead of time, because an unmissable bolt of blue light crashed down behind her out of the clear dawn sky. It was an effect worthy of a hero's entrance.

As Yunyun stood there striking her pose, the thunder still rumbling in the air, I realized that the onlooking Crimson Magic Clan members were weeping.

"...Oh...! ...*Sniff*...!"

Even Megumin had tears in her eyes.

...*Huh?*

Right when I had run out of ideas, everyone else in the village suddenly seemed to be getting excited.

"Yunyun! Yunyun has finally awakened!"

"Yunyun, daughter of our chief, is coming out of her shell at last!"

"Awesome! Yunyun, you're so cool!"

"Yunyun is waking up to the power within her!"

"That's my student! I trained her! That's it, Yunyun, use everything I taught you!"

Yunyun's dramatic display really seemed to have played well with this audience. I had always felt like Yunyun was kind of on her own, but with this, she had been truly recognized as part of the village.

In other words, the one sane girl had fallen from grace.

*   *   *

Yunyun's desire to save everybody had clearly banished her embarrassment for the moment. But I would have to keep an eye on her, because I was pretty sure that when she came back to her senses later and realized what she'd done, she would get so upset she might try to kill herself.

Our newly confident Yunyun stood facing down Sylvia, unflinching. Just for a second, she glanced at the air next to her—but there was nothing there.

"What's wrong, little Teleport-less girl? Secret techniques and special abilities—you Crimson Magic Clan people are all talk. And what are you, their spokeswoman? Where is this secret spell of yours?"

Sylvia's taunt showed she was starting to get impatient, but still Yunyun didn't move an inch. Sylvia started to slither closer. Still, Yunyun didn't budge. Finally, Sylvia coiled up her body and snapped herself straight like a bow, launching herself at the rock where Yunyun stood.

Even more quickly than Sylvia could strike, Yunyun jumped down from the rock and set off at a dash. Sylvia, by now thoroughly vexed at Crimson Magic Clan members getting away from her, shouted, "You think you can run? I won't let you go! I won't—"

Sylvia looked mad with joy at the prospect of the chase, but then, still perched atop the rock where Yunyun had been a moment before, she stopped dead. It was almost as if she had found some invisible thing blocking the way. I squinted to see what was going on, and suddenly two people appeared out of thin air in the direction Yunyun had gone. It was Bukkororii and Soketto.

One of them had been using light-bending magic right up until that moment. And if there were two of them, that meant the other must already be prepared with a Teleport spell.

Yunyun ran up to them. Sylvia reached out a hand, panicked.

"No...! You can't—!"

"*Teleport!*"

*　　*　　*

Bummer for her.

As the Crimson Magic Clan looked on apprehensively, Sylvia began visibly shaking.

"......Heh-heh-heh... Ahhh-ha-ha-ha-ha! So much for the all-powerful Crimson Magic Clan! You're nothing but talk! You haven't shown me any magical power whatsoever! You and everyone associated with you are just a bunch of spineless losers!" She couldn't stop laughing. Was she angry-mad or was she crazy-mad?

The others and I hid at a safe distance.

"Aqua," I said, "she's wide open now. Get ready to fire. You remember that spell you used earlier that left her dress all torn up? We'll compress that and shoot it out of this thing. They only asked us to get the weapon, but I think we can put a nice, dramatic finish on this."

"Ah, my time to shine at last, huh? Sounds good. I love a plum assignment."

There was no call to monologue or give Sylvia any warning. It was her fault for leaving herself open. Aqua nodded, magic at the ready. I used Ambush to conceal our intent to attack and Deadeye to take aim. I pointed right at Sylvia, who was still crowing wildly. Time to show off the skills I'd learned sniping in video games.

"*Sacred Exorcism!*" The moment Aqua spoke, the magic absorber on the back of the rail gun sucked up her magic.

"*Deadeye!!*"

I immediately pulled the trigger that would launch the compressed magic at Sylvia...

...and nothing happened.

"Huh?" I pulled the trigger several times—*click, click*—but the gun didn't look like it was going to shoot anything at all. "Aww, c'mon!" I exclaimed. "What's wrong? Is it broken? Is the safety on or something...?" I gave the rail gun a hearty shake, but it didn't seem to help.

"*Sacred Exorcism! Sacred Exorcism!!*" As I looked at the gun, befuddled, Aqua kept chanting her spell. Maybe it amused her to see the thing absorb her magic.

Hrm. This gun had been serving as a clothesline for who knew how long. It wasn't as young as it used to be.

"Let me have a look. I know how to fix these things," Darkness said, and then gave the gun a solid smack.

Was she really the product of a high-class education and noble breeding?

"If you're going to hit it, try a little higher," I said. "Right—there. Maybe the magic is plugged up inside or something."

"Wait," Megumin said, "is that the weapon? It looks suspiciously like the drying pole Cheekera was so proud of. Anyway, perhaps there is something non-magical stuck in it. Shall I go find a pole to clean it with?"

Darkness continued to pound on the rail gun while Megumin wandered off to find something to help muck out the barrel.

"Hey," Aqua said in the middle of all this, pulling on my sleeve. "Heeey…!" She was pointing at something in the distance.

"What? What is it? Try your magic again. Maybe the last one, I don't know, isn't compatible with this thing or something. Try a different spell this t—"

As I spoke, I followed Aqua's finger to find that Sylvia, eyes bloodshot, was looking right at us.

"Well, now, what are you up to? What have you got there? Such an interesting little toy!"

It was obvious that I was her new target.

8

"Just wait right there, little boy! Set down that thing you're holding and walk away. Call it a Demon King general's intuition, but I've got a bad feeling about that item."

*   *   *

Sylvia's silver body slithered straight for us, completely ignoring the Crimson Magic Clan wizards who tried to hold her back. She seemed to have guessed that my rail gun was dangerous.

What was I going to do? Was there someone I could foist the gun off on?

"Waiiit!" Aqua exclaimed from behind me, Komekko in her arms. "Your stats are so much lower than mine—how come you're so fast when we're running away? Is this what you took the Flee skill for? Wait! Don't leave me!"

Somewhere along the line, Komekko had picked up Chomusuke and was cradling her, just as Aqua was cradling Komekko.

This girl was going to be serious trouble.

"What's going on? Hurry it up! Darkness, you're falling behind— you need to lose some weight!"

"Dammit, don't say it like that! Say my armor weighs too much!"

I didn't know when Darkness had had time to equip her armor, but now it was slowing her down. As she fretted about my choice of words, Sylvia closed in, almost on top of her. This wasn't getting me anywhere! The gun was too heavy. I had to get rid of it...!

"Running won't save you, Kazuma Satou! And you, Crimson Magic Clan, hear this! From this day forth, you may count me your most feared enemy! Wherever you hide, I will find you, and I will squeeze the breath out of every last one of you! No matter where in the world you build your new home, I will come and destroy it!" Her words echoed around the burning village.

If we handed over the rail gun, maybe she would give up on us...

"I tell you, Crimson—or should I say *Coward*—Magic Clan! You and everyone you know shall live the rest of your lives with the ever-present fear of an attack, never knowing when I might strike!"

This failed to get a rise from any of the Crimson Magic Clan wizards, who didn't appear to have taken any notice of Sylvia's threat. From the way they had linked up with Yunyun to the way they used Teleport, I was starting to wonder if maybe these guys had some smarts after all. If only we could get them to put that intelligence to better use.

"My big sister is not a coward!"

A shout loud enough to drown out Sylvia's cackling resounded through the village. It came from Komekko, still holding Chomusuke and still resting in Aqua's arms. It kind of bothered me that Chomusuke looked sort of out of it and appeared to have teeth marks on her, but now wasn't the time to worry about that.

"It is indeed hard to let such an insult pass. This quarrel is between the Crimson Magic Clan and the Demon King. If I give you the weapon Kazuma is holding, will you let these three go?"

If it wasn't our short-tempered wizard, whose boiling point could be achieved with a warm breeze. She had suddenly stopped running and was pointing her staff at Sylvia.

Sylvia slowed at the sight; she licked her lips and smiled.

"Well, if it isn't Kazuma's undistinguished little friend. Come to think of it, I haven't seen you use any magic yet. What's your specialty? Teleport, or some other kind of port?" She smirked.

Megumin responded flatly, "I have not told you my name yet, have I? My name is Megumin. And I am *truly* first among the spell-casters of the Crimson Magic Clan."

Apparently, she was still miffed that Yunyun had tried to steal her title. But she didn't give her name in the usual bombastic way. She spoke calmly and quietly. Sylvia looked surprised.

"You're unusual for a Crimson Magic Clan wizard... No shouting and posing? I know how much your kind loves theatrics."

Megumin didn't so much as raise an eyebrow at Sylvia's taunt.

And in the middle of it all: "My big sis is awesome! She could even blow away a Dark God with her magic!" That was Komekko, still in Aqua's arms.

Megumin glanced at her sister and gave a half smile. "I'm sorry. Please look after Komekko. She would go after the Demon King himself if you took your eyes off her. As for me, I will go use my special magical technique to rid us of this enemy."

"H-hey," I said, trying to stop her, but she paid me no mind—only took off the bandage over her eye. I thought she'd said it would be bad for her if the village found out she could use only Explosion. As I stood there worrying, Sylvia laughed again.

"Ah, the famous 'special magical technique.' How many times have I heard that?"

The other members of the Crimson Magic Clan started whispering, too.

"What's going on? That's Hyoizaburou's girl. She used to have more style."

"If she's going to use special magic, she ought to build up to it a little more!"

"Yeah, where's the pizzazz? The panache?"

They didn't realize that Megumin really did have a serious trick up her sleeve. I had said we were keeping her in reserve, but that was just so our hot-blooded mage wouldn't use her magic where the villagers would see. Megumin was raring to go, but I hated to see her use her Explosion at the wrong moment—to let her secret out when we weren't even sure it would work. Plus, I didn't have any confidence that I could run away while carrying the MP-less Arch-wizard.

"...Hey, Megumin, there's something I have to tell you..."

"Kazuma—"

I was hoping to convince her to hold back, but she spoke at the same moment I did.

"—Aqua told me that...that you can read the ancient letters written in the underground storehouse."

That gave me a shock. Why would she tell Megumin something like that?! For that matter, if she was bringing this up now, it could only mean...

"I'm sorry you always have to clean up our messes," she said with the tiniest of smiles. "Just for today, let me clean up yours."

...These Crimson Magic types really are smart. I finally understand that all too well.

Megumin's eyes shone scarlet. Sylvia looked amused by her.

"Are you ready, little girl? I don't suppose you'll come at me on your own. I'll chase you, and then you'll run away or Teleport or who knows what." There was a challenge in her voice. But our short-tempered wizard listened impassively, her staff at the ready.

Sylvia wasn't the only one who grew suspicious at this. All of the onlooking Crimson Magic Clan members wore dubious expressions.

...We were in for it now. I had never seen Megumin so serious.

I knew how powerful her Explosions could be. The rest of the Crimson Magic Clan was just close enough that they might get caught up in the blast. But hopefully it wouldn't be bad enough to kill anyone. And if Megumin could fire off her spell without causing any innocent casualties, she wouldn't hold back.

"All of you, run!" I shouted. "Get as far away from Sylvia as you can! Seriously, get out of here!" But for some reason, this only provoked an *Ooh* from the assembled crowd.

"That's Megumin's friend for you! He may be a stranger, but he knows how to ratchet up the tension!"

"No kidding... You see the desperation on his face? He doesn't even look like he's acting!"

None of them was taking me seriously...

"You idiots! There's some majorly powerful magic brewing! You have got to get out of here!"

Sylvia—and the whole Crimson Magic Clan—laughed at this. What did they think this was, stand-up comedy...? I gave up trying to convince them—whatever befell these guys wasn't my responsibility anymore. Darkness and I rose to stand beside Megumin.

"Don't worry, Megumin," Darkness said. "If your Explosion doesn't work, I'll hold off that snake lady. Just the thought of those metallic coils squeezing me...!"

"Can you not even keep it together at a time like this?"

"I'll stay as far away as I can—to keep Komekko safe!" I grabbed Aqua as she made a bald attempt to escape. I set the rail gun at my feet and drew my katana.

These antics brought a faint smile to Megumin's face. And then, calmly and quietly, she began the chants for Explosion.

As they caught the sound of her incantation, all the Crimson Magic Clan members, watching from afar, immediately fell silent. That was experts in magic for you. They seemed to know what was going on. Why Megumin had been avoiding drama.

With drawn faces, the Crimson Magic Clan wizards all began evacuating. Sylvia was looking from one of them to the next, unsure of what was going on. For almost a year now, I had heard Megumin's chants every day—more times than I could count. I had a pretty good idea of when she would be finished.

Eventually, perhaps because of the magical power welling up in Megumin or maybe because of the way the other wizards were reacting, even Sylvia seemed to catch on that all that talk about a special technique was no joke. Constantly having her prey escape from her seemed to have left her drained. She almost looked frightened in the face of Megumin's absolute seriousness.

"A secret technique? Pfah! Y-you can explode me, or blow me up, or use whatever high-level magic you like on me! Now that I am one with Mage-killer, I can take anything you throw at me! And when you see that you've failed, then you will all meet your end!"

Sylvia made this pronouncement with both arms crossed in front of her face.

Megumin opened her crimson eyes wide, pouring all her magic into a single spell.

"*Explosion*!!!!"

An overwhelming magical power surged through her staff, blasting out from the tip.

"Wha—?!"

When she realized what spell Megumin had used, Sylvia's face contorted in terror as the light from Megumin's staff lanced out...

...and was absorbed by the rail gun at my feet.

""""""Huh?"""""

We weren't the only ones to exclaim—the other wizards and even Sylvia cried out at this completely, totally unexpected turn of events.

At the same moment, Megumin, her magic spent, collapsed onto the ground.

Sylvia, enraged by the fact that we had managed to actually threaten her, shouted, "Try to intimidate me, will you, you little brat?! When I get my hands on you, I'll tear you limb from limb!"

I guess that was the male part of her talking. She was rushing at us, steam practically coming out of her ears. I guess Hell hath no fury like a Sylvia scorned. I liked her feminine side better!

"Dammit! This stupid piece of junk just doomed us all!"

"K-Kazuma!" Darkness said. "Sylvia's coming! You take Megumin and get out of here. Then come back and rescue me—but maybe let me endure my fate at Sylvia's hands for an hour or so first."

"Dear Kazuma! As a goddess, I must protect this precious little life called Komekko—so I'm getting out of here! Bye!"

Some friends!

"Hey, something's going *bleep bloop*."

*　　*　　*

Komekko suddenly spoke up from where she was cradled in Aqua's arms beside me.

I followed her gaze and noticed that the little display on the side of the rail gun read, FULL.

I thought back to the diary. This weapon compressed magic and then shot it out. It wasn't broken at all; it just hadn't had enough magical power stored up to fire a shot.

I grabbed it, aimed it at Sylvia's onrushing form, and...

"Sylvia, general of the Demon King! When you arrive in the netherworld, say hello to the other generals for me! Remember my name—it's *BOOM*!"

...I delivered the most dramatic line I could and made to pull the trigger. But Komekko, reaching over from where Aqua was holding her, got there first.

The rail gun gave a massive kick, and a bright light burst from the muzzle. Sylvia raised her silver tail as a shield, but the light punched right through it and then through her, leaving a gaping hole in her chest.

Even then, it showed no sign of stopping. The beam of light flew straight on to the sacred mountain behind Crimson Magic Village, colliding with it and knocking off a part of it...

...and with a blinding flash and a deafening roar, the light disintegrated the piece of mountain.

The heat of the shot had twisted the barrel of the weapon. I tossed it aside at the same moment that Sylvia's huge body fell to the ground with a heavy *thump*.

Lying there on the verge of death, Sylvia spat blood and murmured distantly, "...Wh-what? Is... Is this how it ends for me?"

At the sight of her, everyone, even the Crimson Magic Clan wizards watching from a safe distance, stood dumbfounded.

Just then, Komekko jumped out of Aqua's arms and struck a pose.

*   *   *

"My name is Komekko! First among the beguiling little sisters of the Crimson Magic Clan! And she who is stronger than the general of the Demon King!"

Aww, man! She stole my moment!

9

When Sylvia had breathed her last, the Crimson Magic Clan said they would take care of the body. Given that she had merged with Mage-killer, they thought they could put her remains to good use making items that would repel magic. Talk about finding the silver lining.

As for the village, which just that morning had been all but leveled by Sylvia's attack…

"What's going on here?" I said in amazement as I watched things being rebuilt with incredible speed. All the rubble had been cleaned up with magic. Golems had been temporarily made from bedrock, and they were helping with building projects. There was even a six-armed demon that had been called using summoning magic, a carpenter's tool in each of its six hands…

"…Hey, Megumin. What's the deal? How can you rebuild so fast?" The outrageousness of the entire Crimson Magic Clan came home to me again.

"Is this fast? I do not know how long it takes to rebuild other towns, so I cannot say."

"Well, about how long do you think it'll take before the village is completely back to normal?"

"Perhaps three days, I suppose."

Three days?!

A general of the Demon King razes your village, and you put everything back in three days?

"But I saw this girl with a super-sad look on her face going, 'Our village... It's burning...' And I felt really guilty, and—"

"That is most strange. Everyone in the village should know that a few burned-down buildings are easy enough to repair. What kind of person was this?"

What kind...? I'm pretty sure she was wearing a bandage a lot like Megumin's...

"...That's her," I said, pointing at a girl with a covering over her eye who just happened to walk by at that moment.

"What's her?" the girl said. "You want something with me, outlander? 'Sup, Megumin, I've been looking for you."

"Oh, Arue. I have not seen you in a while."

It looked like Megumin and the bandaged girl knew each other.

Wait—Arue?

"Megumin, take a look at this. I just finished it—it's chapter two of the *Chronicle of the Hero of the Crimson Magic Clan*. I'm especially happy with the scene where Crimson Magic Village burns. It's pretty much my masterpiece."

The scene where the village burns...?

Arue...?

I knew that name...!

Wasn't Arue's stupid letter the reason...

"Oh-ho? Let me have a look—"

...we even came here in the first place?!

"It's *youuuu*!"

"Ahhhhhh!"

I grabbed the paper she had given to Megumin and tore it clean in two.

"Ahhh! My... My masterpiece... The gem I pulled a week of all-nighters to craft..."

Megumin patted Arue on the shoulder as she scrambled to collect the scraps of paper I'd dropped to the ground.

"Arue, I thought nothing could move you. I have never seen you like this before."

"This is all your fault…!" I said. "Do you know how eager I was—how overjoyed—and then how devastated?! All because of you! How dare you play with a man's heart like that!"

"M-Megumin, who is this brute?! Is this how you greet someone you've never met before? You're going to give me a heart attack!"

"I'm the one who almost had a heart attack! You and your 'Our village… It's burning…'! As if it really meant something to you! Screw your 'chronicle'! While we were all out there putting our lives on the line, you were shut up in your room writing this junk?! Do you have any idea what heartbreak I suffered because of that stupid story you sent Yunyun?!"

"Stupid story?!"

"Both of you, calm down. How can two complete strangers act so…familiar—? Hey! Both of you! If you insist on fighting, I shall let my newly increased level do the talking!"

10

It was our last night in the surprisingly rapidly rebuilt Crimson Magic Village.

"Kazuma," Megumin said, "what's wrong? You seemed in such a good mood when we were all having dinner together. Then you go out, and when you get back, you look ready to tear someone's head off."

It was true; my face had been stormy since earlier. "What's wrong?! I'll tell you what's wrong! That 'Mixed Bath' down the street? False advertising! It's not mixed bathing! It's not even a bath!"

Megumin seemed to understand what I was saying.

"Ah," she said, "you went there, did you? That building is for tourist use. Every traveler who visits the village goes at least once."

"What is the problem with this village?! Even the bathhouse is like some sick joke! Man! This is the worst trip ever."

Sylvia was defeated, and we had cleaned up the rest of the Demon King's forces in the area. The village had been rebuilt, and everything seemed to have a nice little bow on it...

"Really? I quite enjoyed myself this time."

Megumin rolled over next to me in bed as she spoke. I would really have liked to just sleep quietly on our last night here, at least, but I ended up stuck in Megumin's room again. Yuiyui didn't even have to manipulate everyone. Megumin volunteered—she said it was better than having another Sleep spell cast on her. If she had been that straightforward about it in the first place, maybe I wouldn't have had such a strong urge to sexually harass her.

Darkness voiced her usual objections, and she and Hyoizaburou soon found themselves in dreamland. And I found myself lying in bed next to Megumin.

"Well, good for you. As for me, I mean between the orcs and Sylvia, I seem to be attracting a lot of, y'know, unwanted attention recently."

"It is just coincidence. I have had a similar experience the last few days."

"S-sorry again..."

When I thought about how I had acted, I couldn't quite bring myself to look at her.

Beside me, Megumin snickered.

"If you're feeling guilty, you could... I know. Tell me an interesting story. I'd really like to hear something about your home country." Then she turned toward me...

"...so I thought as fast as I could, and I said to the girl next door, 'Take this money, buy some chocolate, and bring it to my house on the day. You can keep all the change.' It went perfectly. My little brother only got the one chocolate, from our mom. And I got two: one from our mom and the one from that girl. And so the long battle between my brother and me came to an end, and I taught him not to mess with his big brother."

Megumin, who had listened raptly to my entire story, said, "So in other words, you won by paying off a girl. I'm actually glad to know you've always been that way... But what an odd custom. Is it really such a bad thing not to get any chocolates on that day?" She seemed very interested in this, the darkest of days on my country's calendar.

"A bad thing? Let me put it this way. If you told me I had one chance to go back in time, I would find the guy who started that tradition and wipe him off the face of the earth. That's how bad it is for guys who don't get any chocolates. And even if you survive, where I come from, you have to give a gift in return."

"...A gift in return? How does that work?"

I explained to her the awful truth. "So, say you get chocolates from a girl. A month later, you have to give that girl a gift worth three times as much as what you got. How bad is that? And if you don't, it's pretty much social suicide with any girl you know. If you don't give anything to her, she'll point at you and laugh behind your back. But if you do, then you'll end up broke! And that's the story of the terrible event known as Valen-something-or-other."

When I was finished, Megumin cocked her head as if in surprise.

"Why didn't you get any chocolates, Kazuma? It is true you have a number of tremendous flaws as a human being, but even so, I do see good things about you when we're together. For example, you're very... very...kind? No, that's not it. Sincere...? No, not that, either... Huh? Hmm... You're rather skilled at getting along in the world. Wait, but then again, there was all that debt... Huuuh?"

Oh, "huuuh" yourself. Try a little harder. I'm sure you'll think of something.

"...Well, you may be manipulative, but despite everything, you do look out for your friends. I don't hate that about you."

I look out for my friends, huh? Isn't that just what girls say when they don't really see you as a member of the opposite sex? Like "You're a nice person"?

Then again, since I wasn't looking for a love connection here, I guess I didn't really mind. What with the trauma of the orcs and everything with Sylvia—well, anyone would be a bit suspicious when it came to being noticed by someone who looked like a member of the opposite sex. So I didn't care, even if she couldn't come up with a single heartfelt word of praise!

"If I ever go to your country, Kazuma, I'll give you chocolates on that day. You can make sure your brother sees them." She sounded relaxed and friendly, in her own way.

"You weren't listening. I said that on Whatever-tine's Day, girls give chocolates to boys they *like*. If you go around giving chocolates to every guy you're sort of friends with, you better believe they'll get the wrong idea, and then you'll be in trouble. You're kinda cute, so if you were too generous with the candy in my country, people might start thinking you were easy."

In response, she said:

"But I do like you, Kazuma."

She said it so easily, as though it was no big deal.

"Wait, let's go over that again. Say that one more time." I wasn't going to let myself think I had heard something really important when I hadn't.

Megumin, tucked in so just her head peeked out of the covers, gave a strange little giggle. "I don't *not* like you, Kazuma."

"Hey, that's not what you said! My memory isn't that bad!"

This just made Megumin laugh again.

"Kazuma. Hypothetically—"

"What is it? Hypothetically what? I'm ready; bring it on."

Was she about to let the mood take her and confess her true feelings for me? Could it really be? Sylvia was gone; there was nothing that could disturb us tonight.

Megumin seemed to muster her resolution. "**Kazuma, if you could have a…**"

Yes? A what? Go on! Keep talking!

I all but trembled with anticipation. Megumin asked quietly:

"**…a truly great wizard, would you want her?**"

"I Want the Strongest Wizard"

The next morning.

Megumin brought me out to walk around the village. As we went, we ran into Yunyun, so the three of us stuck together. I suspected Yunyun might want to stay in the village a little longer, but she said she was going back to Axel.

Looking around, I thought I could understand why Yunyun might want to get out of town. Since the battle with Sylvia, there was one thing in the village that had changed.

"Oh! Yunyun, **She Who Brings Blue Lightning**! Long time no see. I was just going to go eat. Wanna come with?"

Another girl, about Megumin and Yunyun's age, called out as we walked along. Yunyun turned red and gave a rapid shake of her head. "Oh?" the girl said, not looking particularly offended. "Too bad." And then she smiled, waving as she walked away.

"...Aren't you popular, O **She Who Brings Blue Lightning**? Why not at least have something to eat with her?"

Yunyun, practically in tears, covered her blushing face with both hands. "Stop it! Don't call me that! Why did I ever do something so stupid...?"

Ever since the battle, people had been treating Yunyun completely differently. She was no longer the weirdo with the strange tastes. Now they thought she was extremely charismatic.

A young guy called out to her as he passed.

"Ooh! Yunyun, **Thunder Bearer**! I was just going to go eat…"

"Well, I wasn't! I'm not eating!"

The guy, who also didn't seem bothered by Yunyun's swift and almost tearful refusal, commented that that was too bad and moved on with a wave.

This didn't appear to be some new form of bullying.

"…Aren't you popular, O **Thunder Bearer**? Why not go along, let him treat you?"

"Stop! Please stop! Don't call me by weird nicknames!" Yunyun yelled, covering her face and shaking her head vigorously.

Suddenly Megumin was grinding the end of her staff into Yunyun's cheek. "Stop? I thought you were first among the spell-casters of the Crimson Magic Clan. You cannot usurp my title and then tell me you don't like nicknames! Come on, strike that cool pose again!"

"S-stoppiiit! Megumin, are you still upset about that?! You couldn't let me have it even once?"

In the midst of their argument, I muttered, "Nice to see such good friends…"

Megumin heard me. She looked up and made a pretend-angry gesture with her staff.

"Anyway, we must go! The transport-shop owner has kindly registered Axel as a Teleport destination for us. We should hurry over and do the paperwork so we can get back to town!"

"Hey, wait up, Megumin!" I smiled as Yunyun rushed off after her friend, then I followed them at an easy pace.

…And then two girls about Megumin's age appeared ahead of us.

"Oh! Funifura, Dodonko!"

I wonder what the connection is here…?

"Long time no see, Yunyun and Gimmick Wizard! How are you doing?"

"Ah-ha-ha-ha-ha-ha-ha! The greatest genius in the Crimson Magic Clan and our most ridiculous joke of a wizard, right in one place! The whole village is talking about you, you know."

Megumin, the object of their amusement, leaped at them almost before they knew what was happening.

"That is some way to greet your beloved classmate whom you have not seen in forever!"

"H-hey, we were only teasing! Sorry! We're sorry! You haven't seen us in a long time, either, and you think attacking us is the best way to say hello?!"

"Stooop! How can your grip be so strong?! What level are you? Ouch, yikes! Stop! Violence is wrong!"

Both girls were soon on the verge of tears under Megumin's assault.

…I couldn't guess as to their history, but Megumin seemed to have the upper hand.

One of the girls turned to Yunyun. "…Hey. You were really cool yesterday. I always thought you were, like, weird. But I guess there's another side to you." She couldn't quite meet Yunyun's eyes as she spoke, embarrassed.

"Yeah, I see you in a whole new light now. You were really cool, Yunyun!" Even the other girl joined in.

But given that Yunyun was covering her beet-red face with both hands and fighting back tears, I wished they would stop.

"Both of you seemed, like, headed the wrong way. You know? We were worried about you."

"Oh yeah! Megumin can be sort of childish, and Yunyun always seemed like the type to be attracted to really awful guys. It's such a relief to see you're both doing well."

Smiles came over their faces. I got an oddly warm feeling myself. I was glad that Yunyun, who seemed so alone in Axel, at least had some real friends here at home.

Then Yunyun turned to me and smiled. "Mr. Kazuma, let me introduce you properly. These are Funifura and Dodonko. We used to be classmates. They're my…f-friends!" She seemed very happy about—in fact, almost proud of—it. I bowed and said hello to the girls. They bowed back, seeming a little flustered to be called friends.

"Hi, I'm Kazuma Satou. I'm a friend of Yunyun's—she really does a lot for me. A pleasure."

""Th-the pleasure's all ours!""

There sure were a lot of attractive women and cute girls in this village. It left me unusually uncomfortable. Then again, the two girls looked nervous, too—or was I imagining it?

That was when Megumin decided to drop the bombshell.

"Hey, I know you never meet any guys and are lonely all by yourselves, but I shall have you stop making eyes at *my man*."

"""""?!"""""

It was so sudden that all three of the other girls froze, looks of shock on their faces.

"Wait, what did you just—? So that stuff you said last night about liking me, you were serious?!"

"""""!!"""""

This only astonished the girls more. Dodonko and Funifura, in an absolute uproar, said, "A m-m-m-m-man?! Miss Only-Has-Eyes-for-Magic got herself a man?! Y-you're kidding, right? You mean you like him as a guy friend, right?"

"Y-y-y-yeah, that has to be it. Megumin, you never cared a whit for being popular or anything, and now—a man?!"

Wait a second.

What's going on here?

Yunyun looked every bit as caught off guard as the other girls. "M-Mr. Kazuma, is it true?" she asked in a small voice. "D-did Megumin really...say she...l-l-l...?"

I glanced at Megumin, trying to ask with my eyes how much it was all right to say.

"Oh, do not be so shocked," Megumin said. "Kazuma has formally greeted my parents with a gift of candies. We have bathed together, and recently we have spent every night snuggled up in bed. So you may judge our relationship yourselves."

"""""—‼"""""

Funifura and Dodonko took a step back, reeling.

I guess nothing Megumin had said was technically untrue...

Megumin gave the two girls a triumphant smirk.

".........Heh." She snorted.

"""‼"""

"......Wa— Waaaaaaah! S-so you got a guy, so whaaaat!"

"I-it's not like we care! It doesn't bother us at aaaaallll!"

And with those parting shots, they ran away. The only person left there with us was the stuttering, agitated Yunyun.

"Yunyun, there is somewhere I would like to take Kazuma. I'm sorry, but could you handle things at the transport shop for us?"

"Huh?! Oh! S-sure, of course... But...a-are you two really...?" Yunyun was so scared she almost couldn't bring herself to look at us.

And in a schoolgirlish tone, something I almost never heard from her, Megumin said, "Even if one of us gets a boyfriend, we'll always be friends, right?"

"W-waaaaaah! You hardly ever call me a friend—why now?! I haven't— I haven't lost to you this time, Megumin; just remember thaaaaaat!"

And then off she ran, just like Funifura and Dodonko.

Megumin took me beyond the village limits.

We found ourselves in a quiet spot in the forest, no one else around. All I could hear were birds and insects. Suddenly, Megumin turned toward me.

...Huh? What's the situation here? Wait—is she...confessing her feelings for me? No, she already did that. Didn't she? Did that thing yesterday even count?

Okay, wait. She did just call me "her man" earlier. Or maybe she was just trying to show off in front of her friends…?

Right. Stay sharp, Kazuma Satou! What if you say, "I like you, too—let's start dating!" and she says she didn't mean it that way?

For that matter, do I like Megumin that way?

Pull it together! You can't go getting all confused just because a girl is a little bit nice to you! Am I so easily swayed?!

All these thoughts rushed through my head in an instant, leaving me confused. Meanwhile, Megumin turned to me and began speaking.

"Kazuma… About what I asked you last night—I will ask again. If you could have a truly great wizard, would you want her?"

…What's this about? She said the same thing yesterday night—but what does she mean by it?

I gave her the same answer I had the night before, as nonchalantly as I could: "If you're asking whether I'd rather have her or not—sure, I'd want her."

Megumin seemed satisfied by that answer. "I see… Yes. I am ready, then." And suddenly, she flashed me a smile.

…Speaking as a virgin—as someone who'd never even been on a date—you should definitely give some warning before coming up with a smile like that. We were alone in the woods. She was ready. She was asking if I wanted a wizard. It was all enough to make my heart pound.

Then she spoke the wildly stimulating words, a hurdle a poor virgin would find it hard to overcome. She said…

"I am thinking I will learn advanced magic."

Wait, what?

That brought me up short. "…Come again?"

Had our Explosion-crazy wizard—the one who would have skipped a meal if it meant being able to set off a blast—had she just said…?

Megumin took out her Adventurer's Card. Looking at it fondly, she spoke.

"I have been giving it a lot of thought, even since before Yunyun started calling me Gimmick Wizard. If I had never met you and Aqua and Darkness, I might never have thought about it—just kept working and working on my Explosion. The people of this village are no doubt disappointed in me, as Funifura and Dodonko have made clear... I shall no longer be your burden, Kazuma. Next time, I want to be the one who helps you and our friends. So... So... **As of today, I seal away Explosion**."

And then she smiled at me.

No.

No, no, no, no, no.

"Hey, wait a second. It's true; it would be helpful if you could use advanced magic. But listen. You don't have to 'seal away' Explosion or anything. Some days we don't even go on quests—you could do your daily explosions then. And even if you don't use it most of the time, it will be good to have an ace up our sleeve when we need it! Didn't you tell Yunyun once that you were putting all your skill points into upping the strength of your explosion and making your high-speed incantations even...higher speed or something?"

Megumin snickered at that. "I'm surprised you remember. I have been carefully saving my skill points so I can use them for that purpose at any time... If I release Explosion, it takes all my MP, and I can't use any other magic that day. By the same token, if I use advanced magic, I won't be able to release an explosion that makes the best of my abilities for that day. If I learn advanced magic, I will chant it over and over again, practice so I can be even just a little bit quicker, just a little bit more powerful." She never took her eyes off the Adventurer's Card in her hand as she spoke.

...The words Vanir had said to me before we left town suddenly came to mind.

"Once you reach your destination, a time will come when one of your companions will confide in you about some confusion. What you say may change the path that person takes in life. Think carefully and be sure the advice you offer will leave no regrets."

So this was what he was talking about. *That stupid cheating demon!*

Did he foresee all this? When we get back, I'm going to douse his doorknob with holy water.

But I couldn't shake the vision of Wiz grabbing the knob and bursting into flame.

Megumin was studying her card like it was the most precious thing in the world. Finally, she silently closed her eyes. Then she took a deep breath and opened them again.

She turned away from me, as if she was struggling with something, then handed her card back to me without turning around. There was a slight tremble in her shoulders.

"I'm sorry, Kazuma. Can I make a very...very difficult request of you?"

"...You can't bring yourself to do it, so you want me to push the button to acquire advanced magic, is that it?"

Megumin gave a single nod.

Dumbass...

"Look, think hard about this. We're coming into money, remember? We won't have to bother defeating anyone or doing anything dangerous if we don't want to. We can just hang around the house, blowing up some small fry when we feel like it—everyone just having fun."

"This from the man who once asked me if I wouldn't even consider taking intermediate magic!" Megumin exclaimed. There was another weird tremor in her shoulders, and she pushed the card at me again. I took it without a word.

"...Not gonna regret this?" I said to her back.

"No. I've resolved not to be a burden anymore. If I had been a normal Crimson Magic Clan member, I'm sure I could've kept those orcs from traumatizing you, stopped Sylvia from kidnapping you... I am first among the spell-casters of the Crimson Magic Clan. Wielder of advanced magic! ...Yes. I think I'll go with that from now on. I have more magical potential than Yunyun. Once I can use advanced magic, I shall truly be first. I will not let her take that place from me."

She got it all out as best she could and forced herself to smile.

...Really. Total dumbass.

She loved Explosion more than anything else; she'd given everything she had to it. I moved my finger across Megumin's card.

Who knew you could operate someone else's Adventurer's Card? I wished I'd found out sooner. Then maybe I could have just grabbed her card or Darkness's back when we met and specced them however I wanted.

When I was done, I gave the card back to Megumin. She didn't even look at it, just mechanically returned it to her neckline. Then she glanced back at me.

"Now then, let's all of us go home. You and Aqua and Darkness and me—back to Axel Town! Oh yes, I heard the reward for Sylvia is quite a sum."

"Oh yeah? We'll have to host a little party when we get back home, then." But as Megumin made to leave, I stopped her. "Say, Megumin. Could you let off an Explosion? Please?"

It was a very sudden request. Megumin responded wearily, "...I just don't know what to do with you. Here I have made my resolution, and before five minutes have passed, you are asking me to cast Explosion. I have no idea what you're thinking."

"In my country, we say, 'Never do today what you can put off till tomorrow.' And anyway, I haven't seen a hundred-point Explosion yet. That weapon boosted the one you dropped on Sylvia. Are you going to let your last hurrah be a trick like that?"

"...You do know how to raise a person's hackles. Very well. My final Explosion. I shall show you a blast more amazing than any you have yet seen!"

And with that, Megumin made a show of pointing her staff at a rock some distance away.

"...Uh, not there, Megumin. That's a little too close. Pick something a little farther off. You're going to give it everything you've got, right? Try that rock over there." I pointed to a boulder on the plain just beyond the forest. Megumin cocked her head at my request.

"I do not mind, but you know that is just at the edge of my range, don't you? ...Oh well. Now I shall demonstrate for you, Kazuma, my last—my most heartfelt—explosion!"

And then she smiled—not the way she had earlier, like she was trying to push something away, but a true smile, from the bottom of her heart. She began her chant with real joy. And then...

"*Explosion*!!!"

A brilliant light flashed from the end of her staff, piercing the rock. This was definitely her biggest Explosion ever. There was an ear-shattering roar, along with a fireball of almost unimaginable size. It looked like it could have taken Sylvia down even without the rail gun.

Megumin, looking stunned at the power of her own magic, pulled out her card. She ran her eyes over it, then looked at me with a startling mixture of confusion and irrepressible happiness. Finally, she gave a dramatic flap of her cape, wearing a huge smile, and announced:

"My name is Megumin! Arch-wizard and wielder of Explosion! First among the spell-casters of Axel, and she who will one day master Explosion!"

Now, that was the Megumin I knew.

I hadn't done what she'd asked. Instead, I had put all her remaining skill points into increasing the power of her Explosion.

Did I want a great wizard? What wizard could be greater than our Megumin? Her explosions had convinced generals of the Demon King to fight her. They had slowed down and even destroyed those same generals. I'd like to see any wizard with more sheer combat power than her.

Even more than a great wizard, what I really wanted was...

Looking at me triumphantly, Megumin puffed out her little chest and asked, "How many points for that one?"

No question.

"A hundred and twenty."

A huge smile came over her face.

Epilogue

"Ah! There really is no place like home! I've had enough travel. What was a *hikikomori* like me even thinking, leaving the house like that?"

It felt great to be back at our mansion after so long away. Two major trips in a row were a little too much for someone who was used to staying shut up in his room. Plus, my business deal with Vanir would mean big money soon enough. I wouldn't have to go on any more trips. I wouldn't even have to go outside.

I was thrilled when the people of Crimson Magic Village had insisted that we take the entire reward for defeating Sylvia. The upshot was that I had plenty of funds now.

I'd decided. No more risky stuff. I didn't care who came to me with what sob story.

"Didn't take you long to show what a worthless excuse for a human being you are, huh, Kazuma? I have to admit I find it oddly reassuring. It kind of helps me feel like I don't have to bother trying too hard, either."

"Aqua, that's only because you think he's like you! Don't sink to his level—he's an example to avoid, not emulate!"

Darkness. How rude.

"Let us go easy," Megumin said. "I think this time, at least, Kazuma did a great job. He deciphered the ancient letters, figured out how to use the weapon, and then defeated Sylvia." Megumin seemed uncharacter-istically prepared to take my side.

"It was your magic that defeated Sylvia, Megumin," I said. "I just pulled the trigger."

"Not at all! Without that weapon to turn magic into sheer destruc-tion, I wouldn't have had the power to do it. It was all thanks to you finding that weapon."

We were basically patting each other on the back at this point.

"...Aqua, what do you suppose is up with those two?" Darkness asked. "They've seemed a little weird ever since we got back... Y-you don't suppose that, while sleeping in the same bed, they finally...?!"

"All right, that's enough speculation. Nothing happened! Right, Megumin? We didn't... Hey, aren't you gonna back me up? She's look-ing at me all suspiciously!"

Darkness was giving me a dubious look as Megumin made her way over to Aqua, still not denying anything. She seemed to be interested in something Aqua was holding. Wait—didn't Aqua usually jump right in with some stupid remark at times like this? What was going on? What had she been doing over there on the couch since—?

DA-DIIING!

...

"Just when did you get your hands on a game? Hey, let me play, too. That should be mine anyway—I'm the gamer here!"

"If you want to borrow it, you'll have to give me something in exchange! Specifically, take my turn cleaning the bathroom tomorrow!"

Just as we were fighting over the Game Girl Aqua had brought home, there was a knock on the door and a man's voice from outside.

"Excuse me, is anyone home?"

Aqua and I looked at each other and nodded silently. We crept up to the door...

"Is anyone ho—? Oh, hello. Are you the owner of this m—? Wait, what are you—?! Yikes! Stop!"

"I don't know who you are, but I'm sure you are here to drag us into some new problem! Be gone, troublemaker!"

"Kazuma, Drain Touch him! Drain his HP until he blacks out! Then we'll toss him out of here and pretend we never saw him!"

"What's this all of a sudden?! Kazuma, what are you doing?! Let go of his hand!"

"I understand you do not want any more trouble, but attacking total strangers is not the answer!"

Darkness and Megumin tried to pull me off our visitor, each grabbing a hand.

The person at our door was a butler type, just on the verge of old age. He was breathing hard and keeping a very close eye on Aqua and me.

When Darkness got a look at him, she exclaimed, "Hagen, is that you?! I thought I told you not to come here unless there was a serious emergency. It's not that I don't want you around; it's just, as you can see, I was worried what might happen to you when you showed up…"

Apparently, this guy was one of Darkness's family's servants. But why was she worried about what would happen to him?

…Well, to be fair, you only had to look at what was happening to him right at that moment.

The butler coughed and then, having collected himself, said, "Young Lady, it is precisely such a grave emergency that has brought me here. As it happens—"

Stop! No more problems! No more risks! No more trouble!

I plugged my ears in an attempt to block out what the butler was saying, but Darkness grabbed my hands and pulled them away from my head so I had to listen.

"S-stop that!" I begged her. "I guarantee this has nothing to do with me—and I don't want it to! I don't want to go anywhere, and I don't want to put myself in danger! I just want to relax at home!"

"You know, I'm really worried about how dirty the toilet must have gotten while we were away. I think I'll go clean it."

As I argued furiously and Aqua tried to make an escape, Darkness grabbed us both and turned to her butler.

"What in the world is going on? Has something happened at home?"

"Something of the utmost importance, milady!" he replied. "If things go on as they are, your only assets shall be lost!"

True, it was hard to ignore that.

"What does he mean, Darkness?! Don't tell me—are you going to go flat?! Is this outrageous body of yours going to wither?! I knew you were too hot to be true! You have the money and power to get a magical item that makes your chest bigger—and that's just what you did, isn't it?!"

"What are you babbling about?! My assets are my defensive abilities, and… No, wait! Hagen, how terrible of you! I must have more assets than that…! Megumin, Aqua, I do have *some* good points, don't I?" she asked, on the verge of tears.

"I am more interested in this magical item that makes chests bigger," Megumin said. "Do you have one or not? And if so, please tell me all about it…"

"Kazuma—and you, old guy—you're both awful! Darkness has lots of good points! Like, she's a softy who will give in to almost anything if you cry and beg her for it. And she's gullible enough to believe pretty much whatever you tell her, which is a great way to pass the time when you're bored, and— Ow, ow, ow, ow, owww! Darkness, stop! You'll split my head open! I'm praising you, here!"

As Darkness dug her fingers into Aqua's temples, the butler said, "That is not what I meant! I meant that our household may lose its noble standing and the young lady be reduced to a commoner! And then our all-too-unworldly mistress would have only one conceivable means of supporting herself: selling her unbelievable bod— Eeeyowch! Milady, please, have mercy on these old bones! You shall kill me!"

Darkness, tears in her eyes, was strangling the butler. A letter dropped at their feet.

"…? What's this?"

"It is a letter from the royal family. If you read it, you will understand my urgency. It relates to your Mr. Satou, as well…"

He glanced in my direction as he spoke. *Please, just leave me out of things for once!*

Darkness opened the letter, her face going pale before our eyes. Then she slumped to her knees. Whatever was in that letter, it must have been real trouble.

"…What's the story?" I asked hesitantly, and Darkness gave a start.

"N-n-nothing! It has absolutely nothing to do with you, so—so don't worry about it!"

Suspicious of her sudden change of tone, I held out my hand.

"Let me see it."

"N-no, sorry. I-I'm sorry for dragging you into everything all the time. Just like you said, right? No more problems! So this time—"

"*Steal!*"

"Ahh!"

The letter popped into my hand. Aqua and Megumin came up curiously behind me, and together we scanned its contents…

To the honorable Kazuma Satou, who has rendered such great service to our country by his defeat of numerous generals of the Demon King. We have heard of your most estimable activities and wish by all means to speak with you. Perhaps we could dine together.

The seal of state and the name of the sender came at the end of the letter.

The sender's name was Iris. Even I knew who that was—the king's eldest daughter.

I.e., the princess.

"Kazuma, turn her down! If you make one wrong move with Princess Iris, it could mean your head! If anyone in our party gets out of line, it could create a huge problem! You don't know the first thing about etiquette, right? And you hate being all stiff and formal. Right? So turn her down! I—I know! The Dustiness family can call in some favors with a nice, tasty restaurant someplace, and we can get just our closest friends together to celebrate all your achievements! So...!"

I looked at Aqua and Megumin, and we all nodded at one another.

"It looks like our moment has come at last."

Darkness shook her head furiously, tears flying, and clung to my waist.

Fɪɴ.

Afterword

Natsume Akatsuki, your author—or something—here.

This series reached five volumes practically before I knew it. Including the spinoff, *An Explosion on This Wonderful World!*, that makes six books altogether. We've been publishing at a rush up to this point, but starting with the next volume, I gather we'll settle into a normal pace. I swear it's not because I begged my editor to give me a rest or to let me go have some fun or anything. It's just because I have other work to do. Really.

What other work? Now that they're making a drama CD, I have to write the story! I have to attend meetings for the serialization with Dragon Age that I mentioned!

The fact that I even have this work to do is because of everyone who has supported this series, starting with Kurone Mishima and my editor K, right up to all my readers.

I hope you'll continue to enjoy the series. You all have my deepest thanks!

Natsume Akatsuki

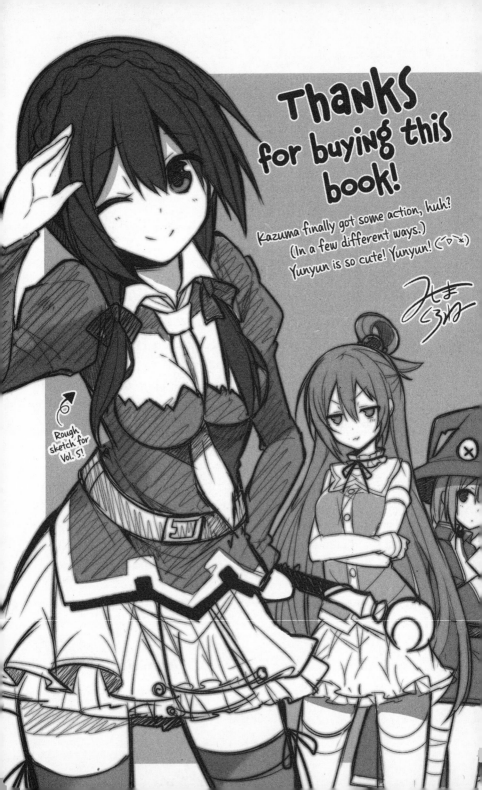

THANKS for buying this book!

Kazuma finally got some action, huh? (In a few different ways.) Yunyun is so cute! Yunyun! (˘▽˘*)

Rough sketch for Vol. 5!

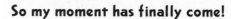

So my moment has finally come!

I—! I have to stop this meeting! I won't let you go to the capital!

Say, Kazuma. Did you ever get those three hundred million eris from your demon friend?

Who cares? What about—?

Yeah, sure did. Plus the reward for Sylvia. I'm filthy rich!

So no need to work, no need to leave the house. You can just—

Let's invite the princess here, then.

??

...What about the magical chest expander?!

I wanna know about that, too, but the capital......

KONOSUBA: GOD'S BLESSING ON THIS WONDERFUL WORLD! 6

COMING SOON!!

Princess of the Six Flowers

Next one's a long one. Will it take place at the capital...or at home?!

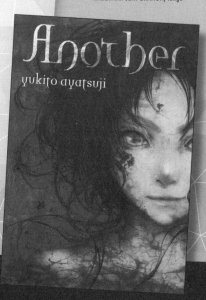

Discover the other side of Magic High School—read the light novel!

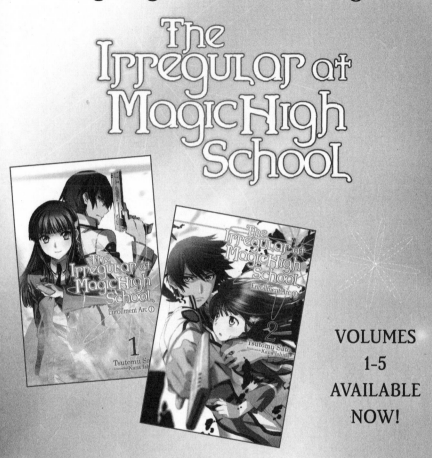

VOLUMES 1-5 AVAILABLE NOW!

Explore the world from Tatsuya's perspective as he and Miyuki navigate the perils of First High and more! Read about adventures only hinted at in *The Honor Student at Magic High School*, and learn more about all your favorite characters. This is the original story that spawned a franchise!